REALITY OF LIFE

Troy L. Palmer

AuthorHouse™
1663 Liberty Drive
Bloomington, IN 47403
www.authorhouse.com
Phone: 1-800-839-8640

Published by AuthorHouse 08/14/2014

ISBN: 978-1-4969-3453-6 (sc)
ISBN: 978-1-4969-3452-9 (e)

Library of Congress Control Number: 2014948585

This book is printed on acid-free paper.

Troy L. Palmer
Aries
(March 21–April 19)

Symbol:	*The Ram*	*Ruling Planet:*	*Mars*
Element:	*Fire*	*Cross/Quality:*	*Cardinal*
Group:	*Emotional*	*House Ruled:*	*First*
Polarity:	*Positive*	*Opposite Sign:*	*Libra*
Colors:	*Real Red and White*	*Lucky Gem:*	*Diamond*
Strong Part:	*Head*	*Belief:*	*What is true*

Overall Grade: B+

The true definition of an Aries: outgoing, dynamic, extravagant, strong, generous, very energetic, sometimes jealous when challenged, insecure, concerned with looks and others' opinions, and arrogant at times.

CONTENTS

PRAYER

Dear Lord, I come today to ask for your blessings once again in life, as sin has been committed and is known to be condemned by your holy hands. Dear Lord, with the highest praise afforded by your grace, we pray for your forgiveness of our most hurtful actions in life. We pray that your hands be placed upon our hearts and minds. Lead us all to the land of glory, where we can praise your holy name forever and ever without false judgment as we celebrate the breath of life you have bestowed upon us all. Good Lord, please help us to continue to grow as one and know our wrongs as we seek the rights of living.

Life is full of unwanted guilt, but in your heart we will shine, and we will be rewarded in life. Together as one we pray, knowing the outcome will be a total reward in your heart. Redemption is what we seek. As your sons and daughters, we pray in your holy name: the Son, the Father, and the Holy Ghost.

Ah-man

ACKNOWLEDGMENTS

The Lord God himself
My wife, Me'linda Rochelle Palmer
My son, Marcus Troy Palmer
My daughters, Empris Ramona
Palmer and Jakia Teasley
My grandmother, bless her soul, Ms.
Lucille Forman (deceased)
My father, Mach Edward Palmer
My mothers, Mortie A. Forman
and Audrey Albert Palmer
My in-laws and my extended family
members, past and present:
Brothers and sisters Courtney, Marcia, Nicole,
Angela, Tabitha, Dionne, Bret, Joshua, Timothy, Carl,
Kashawn, Kawanda, Sylvia, and Shantle (deceased)
Uncles and aunts Glenn, Bonnie, Caroline,
Donisha, Michael, and my Mississippi family
Best friends Charles Roberts and Clarence Lipford
Great friends Dulavian Culver (DC), Rico
Young, Milton Reaves, Edwardo Marcial,
Frederick Burgess, and Derrick Cooper

All of the great US military men and women
I have met and serve with: thank you.

My team, the New Orleans Saints
All Louisiana colleges and universities
Excelsior College
Averett University

The United States Navy and sailors from
all of my former military commands:

USS *Boulder* LST 1190
USS *Sumpter* LST 1181
USS *Harry S Truman* CVN 75
USS *George Washington* CVN 73
USS *George H. W. Bush* CVN 77
Navy Exchange Command
Naval Station, Norfolk, VA

THE CHARACTERS

Mia-Duke "Grahams" Melbourne
Maria Melbourne
Giselle Melbourne
Tulip Melbourne
Rolanda Melbourne Contreras
Security guard
May May Melbourne
Garrett "Studae" Melbourne
Jerry
Mike
Thaddeus "Tricky Tee" Wilson
Jacob "J-Cob" Taylor
Nicole Wines
Joseph John "Jo-Joan" James Jr.
Jesus Rodriguez
Chad
Kathy Jean May
Lakeeba Johnson
Sharon "Shay" Sims
Brittany Jacqueline "Bootsie Jackie" / "BJ" James
Paul Taylor
Robert "Big Bo" McCoy
Liquor store clerk

Kim James
Isaac, Marcia's husband
Marcia David
Mrs. Carroll Jones
Tyrone "Pep" Sims
Derek Sims
Cheyenne Jones
Devin Jacobs
Dee Dee Jenkins
Kyle Dunbar
Travis Mitchell
The Reverend
Tim
New beau of Nicole's
Detective David Dickens
Big Pete
Raul Rodriguez
Todd Morgan
Wilma
Jimmy
Shantel
Marline
Court Clerk
Prosecutor
Defense Lawyer
Judge
Charles Drake
Brianna
Wellington Mitchell
Jone't
Janel

Nasty Boys:
Mr. Tom Wills
Mr. Jake Seamier
Mr. Samuel Miller
Mr. Robert Thompson
Mr. Gregory August
Derrick Jones
Bobby Matthews

Quotes of Life

Smiles are meant to enlighten the heart. Have you smiled today?

CHAPTER 1

THE BEGINNING

Cheyenne (from the living room, in Spanish): Mia-Duke, what are you cooking? Man, I cannot wait. I know it's going to be good.

Grahams (from the kitchen): Thank you, baby, but does your mother ever cook? Lord save me.

Cheyenne (smiling): Okay, Grahams, I get it. I see you are trying to keep a sister hungry.

Grahams: Girl, if you know what is good for you, you would zip it up and wait. Patiently. Wait!

Giselle (from the living room): Pep, baby, when are you going to get up off your butt and get a job? Gosh boy, do you want anything out of life? I just do not know about you young ones these days. I just do not know.

Derek (rambling): Man, why do mommas trip, dog? I thought we answered that question yesterday … (Laughing)

Giselle: Slow down, li'l boy. What is your problem? Do you not realize whom you are speaking too? I am not one of your homeys. I am your aunt, and that gives me the right to slap you silly. What do you mean, you thought we settled this conversation yesterday? How about I fix you? Get up, get your behind out, and get a job! *Dog!* Now do not say word, Pep, or you're next, do you hear me?

Giselle: Mom, I got a letter today from Aunt Wilma. She said she has been trying to reach you, but you keep ignoring her letters.

Grahams: Baby, I am not for talking all that noise with your aunt Wilma. She knows the deal, and that is that. I will deal with Wilma when the Lord tells me to. For now, baby, just let her know that I am praying daily for everyone—I mean everyone.

Jesus: Yo, homes, I told you about your big lips. You can never keep them big boys closed. You're going to learn, bro; you're going to learn. Listen peeps, it has been a pleasure visiting today, but I have to go. I have a lunch date.

Grahams: Boy, sit down and stop running the streets so much. You are always gone. You run out this house at the same time daily. I will keep an eye on you, Jesus. I know your mother. Don't let me get on that phone, son.

Jesus: Yes, ma'am. I understand. But I am not into doing anything illegal. In fact, the young lady I am seeing is special to me, Grahams. I will bring her around one day so you all can meet her. So with that said, I am out ... (Runs to the door.)

Grahams: Lord Jesus, help me and these kids today, I swear. What are we going to do, Lord?

Maria enters the house without speaking, showing attitude and heading to her room.

Giselle (with a frown): Wait wait wait, li'l girl. Just wait there one minute. Where in the hell are your manners? Never enter a house without speaking. And by the way, Miss Melbourne, where in the world have you been all day?

Maria: Giselle, why are you on my back? Lord!

Giselle: What did you call me, young Maria? I am your mother, and you will never address me by my first name. Do you hear me? And if I want to ask questions of you, you will stand there and answer. Do you hear me, Maria? Do you? And you have the nerve to use the word Lord ... Child, please stop playing with the Lord.

Grahams: Baby, calm down. The Lord is watching—yes, he is watching. She will come around one day; she will realize one day.

Maria: Come around where, Grahams? I'm grown. I do not need any guidance. I can take care of myself. Hell, it seems that I have been doing all right from where I stand. Take a look at all this here.

Grahams: Baby, do not sass me. I am not your girlfriend. I started this family; do not make me take from it. Lord, walk with me (singing and walking away).

Maria walks off without comment to her room and Pep starts playing his CDs and dancing. Cousin Tulip enters the front door, loud, clean, and drunk as ever and hears the song, then starts dancing.

Tulip: Your turn, li'l boy. You can't hang with Unk, can you? You don't know 'bout this. (Loudly) Come on, boy. Come on now, get up. Do this, yeah now. Can't keep up, can you? Come on. Do it, Pepper-Snapper. Come on, do it!

Grahams walks over to the CD player and stops the music.

Grahams: Tulip, please sit down and stop that noise. You're going to wake the dead if they ain't awoke already from the smell of alcohol. You need to find the Lord and stop.

Tulip: Stop! Come on, Momma, I have not even had a drink yet. Look at me: not one drop of dirt.

Giselle: I do not know how you can drink so much and stay so clean. What's your secret? Or do you have detergent in your bloodstream?

Tulip: Why do you people always have something to say to me as if I am the only one having drinks in this world? Not that it would be a problem (with a small laugh). I am the— Where's my cane? Pep, boy, get my cane so I can go and be the player I am. Oh, like I was saying, I have not been drinking.

Grahams: Boy, sit down and get some dinner before your liver explodes. Sit down now.

Tulip: Okay. Cannot pass up my momma's meal, never have and never will, because I am a player, a player I am . . . (singing).

Grahams (staring at him with a solid glare): Tulip, shut up now.

Grahams puts on some gospel music.

Derek: Grahams and Aunt Giselle, we will be back. We have to go to the, the, the— Man, help me out. Come on, Pep.

Pep: We have to get out of this house with that music. Dog, be for real and be a man, fool.

Grahams: Be Christians and sit down. Dinner's almost ready. Sit, boys. Sit.

Maria comes back into the room, having changed her clothing, and is ready to go out again.

Grahams (laughing): Child, where are you going now, dressed like some broke fast-tail girl?

Tulip: Now Grahams, leave my baby alone. She looks just fine—yes, just fine. Come give Tulip a kiss.

Maria: You can keep your dry-drunk lips to yourself. I do not play with Mr. Two Lips.

Giselle: Watch your mouth, li'l girl. That is your uncle. You are not on your own yet, so don't stand here and get a free ticket to being there.

Grahams: Family, calm down and sit, all of you, especially you, Maria. It's dinner time, and you looking hungrier and hungrier every day. Besides, you're on my time, not your girlfriends'.

Cheyenne: Maria, when are you going to let me hang with your crew?

Maria: When you ready, sis. All you need is some fly gear, not those Baby Gap rags.

Cheyenne: Child, please. I just wanted to hear what you would say. I don't want to hang with your loud crew. Lord, in fashion and your lips—

Maria: "Get it get it," chick! Now all right, tramp, don't play me, okay?

Cheyenne: Tramp! Okay, I am not the one that Grahams said looks like a broke tramp, so shut up, Maria!

Maria: You better go home and eat, Cheyenne, before you get hurt.

Grahams: For the last time, people, stop rushing my blood. Eat and enjoy. Does the food smell good? If so, talk about good things or shut up.

Tulip: Let me get a drink while I eat. Pep, go fix it.

Giselle: Fix him a glass of water.

Jesus: You might wanna watch Pep. He's the one to watch, not Uncle Tulip.

Giselle: Boy, what is your problem? Do you not see your uncle falling in life? Does your mother, Rolanda Melbourne Contreras, know what has been going on with your drinking?

Pep: Ah, Auntie, it's not that serious. I only sampled a few. I am not hooked on that stuff.

Maria: Pep, you are drinking now? Way to go, li'l cuzz. Handle your business.

Derek (angrily): Don't praise him! When he drinks, he is a trip. You need to stop.

Pep (hesitantly): I do not know what you are talking about. I fixed you a couple last week and you didn't complain.

Derek: Man, stop playing with me and just admit it. You have a problem, and it's not me.

Grahams (puts her fork down): Baby, do you have a problem? Please let me know. I will do all I can to help, and you know that.

Derek: Why are you out here killing yourself, Pep? You are happy, right?

Grahams: Baby, take some time to pray for help. The Lord is watching. Lord, please watch over my grandson. Please, Lord.

Maria: Man, Jesus, why did you have to make my granny sad at the table? Boy, what is your problem? You ignorant punk!

Grahams: Okay, now that is it for the name calling. Baby, I am not sad at this moment. I am praying for his well-being, and do not call names at the table. Pray with me sometimes—all of you pray sometimes. It is refreshing and most definitely a blessing.

A few moments of silence, and Mia-Duke is sensing that a prayer is in the works.

Giselle: Now, after that moment, who wants seconds?

Tulip: Woman, do not ask the question if you cooked. But if not, I want some more (laughing).

Everyone laughs and has a reasonable conversation.

CHAPTER 2

THE PORCH

Maria, Dee Dee, and Shay are sitting on the front porch.

Shay: I have to let you two hoochie girls know that my man has promised me some Timbs for my birthday. Dang, I have a good man.

Dee Dee: Don't even try it! What man?

Dee Dee (laughing): Girl, please stop dreaming. That fool of yours isn't nobody's man; he's everybody man, if ya know what I mean. Right, Maria?

Maria (standing up): Trick, please, do not hate on Shay because you're lonely. It is not her fault. It is yours because you let him hit it back then. Right, Shay? (Laughing.)

Shay: Why bring that up, Maria? I forgave Dee Dee a long time ago. She made it clear that it was a big mistake, and well before we realized who I was interested in. Please don't you trip, Trick. And don't trip because you have a private secret with your girl, Bootsie Jackie. Do not think we do not see it, Trick. Are you down with that, Maria?

Maria: Whatever, Miss Unhappy. I am all female, and you can't handle that, so get gone, girl. Besides, I know the deal. Do you?

Shay: What is that supposed to mean? Are you saying you know something you are not telling? What is it?

Maria giggles under her breath, knowing a secret of Shay that no one else does.

Dee Dee (walking toward the sidewalk): Okay, okay, whatever. Oh hey, Paul, what's up? How long you been standing there?

Paul: Not long, love. I just walked up behind you girls. By the way, did I miss something? Hey, my love (to Maria), my one and only that I am so proud to be a one-woman man.

Dee Dee (under her breath): Oh Lord, what planet you on? I see who the fool is in this relationship …

Paul (with red eyes): What did you say, girl? Don't play with me! What?

Maria (laughing): She didn't say anything, love. What's up, and why are you here so early?

Paul: Not much at work today, so I thought I'd come over and see my girl.

Dee Dee and Shay (exiting): Whatever. Later.

Tulip comes strolling down the street, almost free of wind (out of breath).

Tulip: Baby girl, where's your mother?

Giselle (looking from the window, having observed the entire girl-girl conversation): Tulip, what is wrong?

Tulip: Gangs. Them fools at it again. I lost on of my brand-new shoes running from that bull … I saw Pep over there by the store. Jo-Joan and he were talking, and Jo-Joan seemed to have something on his mind and seemed really sad. The gang members were laughing, and then they stopped and everyone started running away. You know what that meant. Studae and I was out …

Tulip is also keeping a secret, because Studae is sipping on the side.

Giselle: So they scared you out of your shoes, right?

Tulip: Girl, don't play with me. No one scares me. (Looks back,) I am the man.

Grahams (walking up from behind Giselle): Is that true, son? You were scared out of your shoes, I hear. For what?

Tulip: Grahams, not at all. I am Thomas "Tulip" Melbourne.

Giselle: If not your shoes, then it must have been your liquor, because your butt is not drunk.

Tulip (calmly): Okay, I see you have jokes, woman. Anyway, listen, let me get twenty, and I will look out for you on payday.

Giselle: Okay, now I am a fool. Carry on, brother, and get gone. You really think I am a fool or something.

Tulip: Oh, okay. Now don't forget that I was there for you back then when I was on top. Now I am down, you want to keep your foot on my throat. I got you.

Paul and Maria come into the living room.

Giselle (sarcastically): Ha, ha, ha. If it ain't one of the Rodriguez boys.

Paul's brother Jacob, street name J-Cob, is in the neighborhood gang.

Paul: Good evening, Ms. Giselle, Ms. Grahams.

Grahams: Hello, baby. How's your family?

Paul (softly): They are all doing fine, ma'am, and you are looking happy as ever.

Giselle (angrily): Okay, boy, I have heard all that I am going to hear of this. What about these gangs and keeping my daughter out late night?

Paul (smiling): No, ma'am, I am not into gangs. I have no idea what you're talking about concerning her being out late. She told me she was checking in early since she didn't feel so good. That is why I came home early from work to see if my girl was okay. So what is up with that, Maria?

Maria walks off with an "I am sorry" look on her face. She takes Paul's hand and turns to him.

Maria: Look, boo. I said that because I wanted to hang with the girls. You always want me to stay home and become a dating housewife, and that's not me, boo. I am into having fun.

Paul: (angrily): Okay, now I am being played, and it's not my fault. How could you lie to me? I have never done such a thing to you. That's wrong, love. I do love you, but you want to play and hang out. Well, if you are not into the Lord as I am now, how could you be into me? I am the one who's sorry. I know you are still holding me being with Shay against me. It's cool. I'm out of here if you want it that way.

Maria: Who cares? I do not. I can get whomever I want. If you do not want a part of me, then stroll on, love. (Looks at Grahams.) It is me who matters. It's all about me, boo. Bye-bye.

Paul walks away and leaves the house, sad and angry about losing his love, Maria.

Grahams: No, child, you're wrong. It's the Lord who matters. I think you have messed up a real good thing, baby. I hope you reconsider and apologize, because that boy is a good young man and you're the one who can't see. Lord, please save my baby.

Maria (walking toward the back door): No, Grahams. It's about what I want in life, and that's not to be tied down to one man at this point. I am young and I have needs.

Giselle: Baby, slow down. I can't be there all the time for you. One day you'll see. You will see …

Maria: Whatever, Mom. I am a big girl. I know how to take care of myself. I'll be okay.

Tulip (walking up): That's my baby girl, spicy as ever. She's a real young lady.

Giselle: Your butt might just be drunk after all. Shut up, man! Stop backing that li'l girl up all the time, Tulip. Gosh, she is not right.

Dee Dee and Shay blow the horn in Shay's mother's SUV, *beep beep*. Maria shouts from the window, "I am coming," and runs. She gets in the car, and then they head to the mall. No more than thirty minutes after arriving, they are taken by the arms and escorted by security for stealing cheap clothing.

Security Guard: Come with me, young ladies. You have been caught on camera stealing.

Maria: What the hell you mean, stealing, man? I am not a thief, nor are my friends. Take your damn hands off me, man, before someone gets hurt. Move, move, move—let me go, fool!

Giselle: I don't know what's gotten into your behind. Stealing? I have money, girl. If you needed something, all you had to do was ask.

Maria: All I need is to get out on my own and live like a real woman lives, Mom. I was not the one who stole.

Giselle: You may not feel as though you need me, young lady, but until I release your butt into the streets, you are still under my rules. You are going to understand what is waiting for you out there. You'll see what I am talking about one day.

Maria: Mom, I can take care of myself. What am I, some kind of silly kid? Come on. I can handle myself pretty well. I know right from wrong; at least you taught me that.

Gisele: Nah, baby, you don't really know. Like I said before, you'll see. Mark my words with your smart ass. And by the way, get to your room.

Tulip comes from the bedroom, a little woozy

Tulip: Pookie, Pookie Pookie, where the hell are you? I know you're in here. Don't play me, girl. Don't play me. Where ya at? Making me mess up my gear. I am to clean to lean. Come here, Pookie. It's time to play Speed Racer, man, and remember the way they said *speed*, *speed*, *speed*! Come here, girl.

Grahams: Boy, I know you don't have some freak in my house. What's your problem, fool? Stop all of that noise and go to bed. Lord, save him.

Tulip exits to the back room, staggering.

Maria is taken to court by her mother. There is no proof other than the cameras showing the girls reaching in and out of their handbags, and no items were retrieved during interrogation. The judge nevertheless hands Maria the punishment of counseling and probation because of Maria's mouth and her inner anger. He sends Dee Dee and Shay home with no punishment and apologizes to their parents for the big mistake.

The week after the court appearance, Cousin Derek arrives to take Maria to the counselor's office. Gisele directs him to Maria's room.

Maria: I told you not to come. I was going to have Shay take me. I don't want to go with you anyway, man.

Derek: Just shut up and say thank you sometimes. It's not hard.

Maria: Whatever, man. Whatever.

CHAPTER 3

COUNSELING

First session. Devin Jacobs is the counselor.

Devin: Good evening. You must be Maria. How are you doing?

Maria: Yes, and I would like you to know that I don't need counseling, I am just fine, as you can see. Look! The court sent me to counseling; it was not my intent, okay?

Devin: Yes, if you say so. Hey, how about you have a seat and let's get to know one another. Let's talk …

Maria: Look, man, don't try to pick my head like I am some kind of fruity. I am okay. I just told off some rent-a-cop, and it landed me here in your office. For what? My girls and I did not steal anything.

Devin (with a glazed look): What this outburst is going to do is delay the completion of the few session you were assigned by the judge. Please calm down and get it together. Now why do you think you don't have a problem? Why are you so stubborn?

Maria: So happy, mister, not stubborn. I am just a young lady trying to survive in this world, and that's the way I am going to remain until I reach my goals.

Devin: Okay, now we're getting somewhere. You have goals. Go on.

Maria: Yes, mister, and they don't include counseling, which I am still not feeling.

Devin: Well, Miss Maria, in order to have a goal, you have to have needs, and needs require wants. And let me say that if you want something in life, you have to go and get it. You're off to a great start. But you have to control your anger. Become more relaxed toward the world. Focus on the positives and less on the negatives. It's there if you want it.

Maria: Is this session over? It's been fifteen minutes. I was only assigned a half-hour session per week for one month. But if things are going to go this way, I think we can save each other a lot of time and end here. Good-bye, counselor!

Devin: Okay, young lady. Let me say that this isn't the time or the place. (Begins to sing "Not the Time, Not the Place" by Marvin Sapp.)

Marie: Whatever, man. Whatever! Bye-bye.

As Maria leaves, her phone rings. It is her transvestite friend Jo-Joan, who has been going through a lot lately with her/his family as they find out the truth of his lifestyle. His father has disowned him. His mother loves him but cries daily over losing her one and only son. Instead of a boy and a girl, she now has two girls. She prays and prays, only to remain sad as nothing changes in Jo-Joan's life, whose real name is Joseph John James Jr.

Jo-Joan: Hey, Maria. Girl, how are you, and where have you been for the past half hour? I've been calling you and calling you. Dang, girl, I have so much to tell you. My heart is hurting, my brain in numb, and my life is in shambles. I am so pissed.

Maria: Girl, shut up and slow down. How in the world do you expect me to register all of this at one time? Okay now, first things first. What's up?

Jo-Joan: Girl, I went to the club last night, and my guy friend was all hugged up with another tramp. A girl at that! How can he hurt me like that? And to top it off, my family didn't care one bit about my tears last night as I entered the house. My father hates me. My mother is still in disarray. And my sister is an A-hole as always. What can a girl do? I am in need of so much right now. I have sat and thought over and over about what I can do. I have sometimes thought of ending it.

Maria: Wow! Slow down, girl. What you mean, ending it? Jo-Joan, I think you need to speak to someone. Hell you seem to need the counselor I just left! Or attend a group meeting for individuals in your lifestyle. To me it is not hard: either your family accepts you are they don't. What are you supposed to do, act straight when you are not?

Jo-Joan: Girl, I just don't know. I am so sad. I want my family to accept me for me and not disown me because of who I truly am in life. I love who I am, Maria. I do, and I am not going back to being miserable.

Maria: Listen, girl, it will be okay. I know it may be hard. Hell, I feel that my life is hard right now too, but I am Maria. I will always do what I want to do, and no one can stop me. Ya heard me! And listen to this carefully: I would never hurt myself. Never!

Jo-Joan: No one can stop you? Oh, child, someone can and will if you don't watch out. I was stopped the other day from hurting someone or getting hurt as this gang of dudes was harassing me as I left the store. I mean, all I was doing was getting me a drink, and all of a sudden I became the most hated girl in the world. They called me so many names ... (Crying.) I was so ashamed of who I was and just stood there and let them belittle me.

Maria: Oh, girl, I am so sorry you had to go through that. People are so closed-minded in life.

Jo-Joan: Yes, they are. But get this: just when I had enough and was about to run off, your cousin Pep walked up and put his hand in his pants and told all them bastards to shut up. They looked at him with rage in their eyes. Then they looked down at his hand in his pants and backed off and ran away. I gave Pep a hug and told him thank you, and of course he pulled away. But I didn't care because he stood up for me, a gay guy name Jo-Joan—and girl, you know Pep is one cute guy! Across the street, Tulip and Studae were arguing because Tulip wanted to borrow money and Studae said no. Tulip is always bumming. They observed the entire scene, including the hug. They didn't know what to think. They seen Pep reach in his pants as he spoke to the gang members, and they ran away toward Mia-Duke's home.

Maria: What? Pep had a gun? What in the world …

Jo-Joan: I don't know. He never pulled it out. Oooo child, pulled it out! I am so funny. But do you think he is packing? I mean, packing a weapon? Lord, let me stop … (Laughing.)

Maria: Shut up, Jo-Joan. You crazy. But seriously, you are okay, right? I mean, you are not still having feelings of hurting yourself?

Jo-Joan: Nah, girl. I guess every gay person goes through emotional trips from time to time. It's just hard trying to understand life and getting others to understand your pain or happiness. I am happy in many ways, just not with my family at this time. I would never hurt all of this. (Turns around and sashays.)

Maria: Jo-Joan, you go 'head, girl. I know you are strong and wouldn't stoop so low in life. Suicide is a cop-out to me. It is not the answer to people's problems. It is a start of others' pain. People don't know how many are hurt by the loss of a loved one. Suicide makes other people think they were the cause of the dead person's issues. Life is precious. Make life work for you. Hell, I am … (Laughing.)

Jo-Joan: Maria, girl, you are so right, but why do you always seem to get in trouble?

Maria: My mouth, girl, and mostly because my family and some associates are straight haters. (Snaps her fingers.) But I'm good! Hey, girl, look; I gotta go, so please call me anytime. I am here for you. And oh yeah—you are going to the party this weekend, right?

Jo-Joan: Yeah, girl. You know I will be there with my gear in order. And hey, Maria, ask Pep what is up.

Maria: I'd rather not. Your butt might get blasted.

Jo-Joan: Yes, a weapon … (Laughing.)

Maria: Nah, fool, get cursed out. Bye, Jo-Joan.

Jo-Joan: Bye.

J-Cob, the guy with a lie, has been creeping up his secret ladder, all the while covering himself by being in a gang. He is really on the down low. While doing a three-year bid for assault, he started feeling lonely and resorted to sleeping with a prag (the word homosexuals are referred to by in prison).

J-Cob has been going through an identity issue since being released. He set out to recapture his manhood, only to find himself back in the arms of his prison partner, Jo-Joan, who was sent up for shoplifting. Jo-Joan has fallen in love with J-Cob and can't let go of his feelings. J-cob tries seriously to move on with a new interest, a female named Lakeeba, who has been a constant headache to many in life.

At the club:

J-Cob: Hi, Lakeeba. Girl, what's cooking? Damn! You look good in them jeans.

Lakeeba: I know, and I don't need any compliments from a man I know as an asshole who wants to run with his boys, causing havoc daily. I want a man who will look at me and say, "My love, you are looking so sweet this evening."

J-Cob, laughing with his boys, looks and starts playing, although he is soft as a pillow at heart and really feeling Lakeeba. His laugh causes Lakeeba to react. She goes to slap him for taking her as a joke. Her swinging hand is caught, and she is pulled into J-Cob's arms. He kisses her on the lips at the same time that Jo-Joan enters the club and looks straight at them. Jo-Joan is hurt and immediately leaves the club, crying and heading to speak to his one good friend, Maria.

Lakeeba breaks free of J-cob and slaps him. Then she walks out the club and heads home.

J-Cob laughs it up with his boys, knowing that as he planted a kiss on Lakeeba, it was a ploy to distract Jo-Joan, who has been demanding that J-Cob open up and express his love for Jo-Joan.

Drinks are ordered, and J-Cob and his boys live it up for the night. All the while, a deep pain of regret has set in for J-Cob. Being down low is really starting to take its toll, and the fact that he is preaching and bragging and ranting slurs at the same people he is really one of deep down.

Life is too short to live unhappily. He really feels it is time to be free and who he is in life. But can he handle the anger of many who have befriended him since his release from prison, including his father Chad?

Chad has sat at home with his boys and preached a sermon about how he despises men who play the dangerous game of sleeping with women and men, with all the diseases arising these days. His anger toward down-low men is so strong that he has been heard saying he would kill one of them if they ever crossed paths with his daughter. He has always resented the pain he caused his daughter and her mother by his drinking. He has never been a good man and is one for the streets, but he wants badly to rekindle his love with Kathy, his only wife.

Chad's unfaithfulness caused Kathy to run into the arms of a man more stupid than he was. But he wants a life with his daughter. He has vowed the day will come when he will find her and show her. He will also defend her honor in ridding any down-low man of the joyful feeling of living. The question is where Kathy is. He's heard she's run away from the pain of the man whom Chad has vowed to make pay for hurting his one true love, Kathy.

Lakeeba is embarrassed and mad as hell. She leaves the club, never wanting to see J-Cob again. But deep down, she loved the kiss. It was rough but passionate, and confusing from a man who wants to viewed as a hardhead but is really sensitive in his true spirit. Lakeeba has not slept with J-Cob, but the interest is there if only he lightens up and starts treating her with respect.

Lakeeba heads to her spot and calls Maria. Maria has been on and off the phone for hours, ranting about her issues, ignoring all and whoever calls. She finally answers with an attitude.

Maria: What up, girl? You know I am a busy woman. What you mean, this fool J-Cob kissed you? I think you better wash your lips if you ask me. Paul has been really tripping on his brother, and for some reason, he is not feeling him at all. They barely talk. Who cares anyway? I am not for talking of Paul, who is tripping and doesn't respect me for who I have become. He makes me sick.

Lakeeba: Look, Maria, I called you for help, and this is what I get—your issues. I can never open up to you and have you listen to me. Girl, stop and listen. I am hurting and confused here. Damn!

Maria: Look, chick, we all have problems. Yours is being confused over a dude who is confused. I would steer clear of that fake gangster if ya know what I mean.

Lakeeba (laughing): I get you, girl, and I am sorry. I just like him so much, but he is always playing hard and shit for no reason. But girl, get this. You know your friend Jo-Joan was sitting outside on the corner, crying like she just lost her best friend. I know you and her are cool and all, but why was she tripping and crying? I thought she was in control. To let some fool break her down is a crying shame. Well, I guess a man does cry in the dark. (Laughs again.)

Maria: Girl, shut up. Damn, hold on. I have a call coming in. (Looks at her caller ID.) Look here, Lakeeba, let me get this, because it is Jo-Joan. If you say she was crying, I need to get the footage. Holler! (Clicks over.)

Quotes of Life

The true spirit is the given thought.
Think before you act.

CHAPTER 4

MAY MAY

Back at the house, Aunt May May comes to visit.

Knock knock.

Grahams: Come in.

May May: Hi, Mia-Duke, how's my mommy doing? Oh, Lord, it's great to see you, Mother.

Grahams: Hey, baby, how you are doing? Sit down and relax your feet. Now, baby, what brings you here today?. Are you still with that man?

May May: Honey, I just really needed a break from my hectic schedule, that's all. I am too old to be yelling all day. Whew. Lord.

Grahams: Well, baby, everyone needs a break. It's your time, so take all the time you need to get things together. It's not going to take too long, right? Lord save me!

Giselle comes into the house. She and May May haven't seen eye to eye for years.

Giselle: Lord, what have you dropped off today, my baby sister? What in the world no-calls we just pop up now in life. Like some teen popping up pregnant! (Hint hint.) First things first. How long are you staying this time, and whose fault is it also, yours?

May May: Girl, don't start. I am here, and Mommy's happy to see me. Now what and what!

Tulip and Kim, his drinking buddy, comes through the door, both woozy.

Tulip: Hey, li'l sis. How you doing, and what brings you into this house again? Your man? (Laughs.) Just playing. But why are you here anyway? Your man, ha ha ha.

Grahams: Lord please save him. Please.

Giselle: Girl, no. He didn't bring that thing Kim, the public nuisance, in this house.

May May: Yes, he did. What in the world is his problem, always drunk?

Kim: Hey y'all! My boy came to the shot house and got me. Now that is a friend. (Crying.) He says Grahams wants to see me and she cooked me a real nice meal. Where you at, Grahams baby?

May May: Not in my mommy's house. Back up and hold it till tomorrow or when you leave. Drunks.

Grahams: Gisele, shut up, child. Now, Kim, sit down and let me feed that liver. Tulip, you should be ashamed.

Tulip: Mother, what I do now?

Grahams: Okay, Tulip, zip it, now!

Tulip; Yes, ma'am.

Later the next evening, the Melbourne family awakes to crying on the back porch. It is Maria. She is drunk, as she has turned to the bottle. She's been introduced to this world by a new friend named Raul, in town from Mississippi.

Grahams: Baby, what is wrong? Why are you so unhappy in life? Why have you become so hateful? Why? Lord, please help my baby. She knows not what she does these days. Please help her.

Maria: I am all right, Grandma. I am all right. I am just a little tipsy, nothing more. Just look. I am still cool. Look.

Grahams: Pep, please put that girl in her bed before I whale off and hit someone. My Lord doesn't want that of me; I know he doesn't.

Pep: Yes, Grandma. I will. Come on here, little big fool. You're always starting something.

Maria: Because I can, and don't think I don't know about your secret, fool. I do. Now you want me to tell Granny about that, huh? You better shut up before me. (He covers her mouth with his hands.) Mu muumuu. Get your hands off of my mouth, boy. Mommy! I'm going to tell. Leave me alone, Pep. Stop.

Pep looks worried and heads straight for the door. He doesn't know what Maria knows and is becoming really edgy.

Pep: Bye, Grahams. I will be back later. I'll see you then.

Grahams: Baby, I am about to cook breakfast. Where are you going, Pep? Lord, these kids today. Help them.

Pep passes his cousin Studae on the way out.

Studae (stuttering his words): What's up, people? Grahams, baby, I am hungry. Can I please join this lovely occasion?

Grahams: Boy, please sit and shut up. Lord, help my grandbaby, please.

Tulip: Boy, shut up, because Uncle Tulip don't want to laugh while he eats. Whatcha cooking, Mommy? I sho' is hungray.

Grahams just gives Tulip one of her staredowns, and he quickly takes a seat.

Studae: Uncle Tulip, you're so funny. Man, I love to come over here just see you drunk. Hey, excuse me, but are you drunk, right, sir?

Tulip: Boy, I know my mom told you to shut up. Let's make it happen, Studae. Make it happen.

Jerry, a family friend, comes over to say hello. He has a crush on Maria, but she doesn't know it.

Jerry: Good morning, my other family. How's everything going? Where is my Maria? I have to speak to her. I must. Oh, my God, hello, Mother Grahams. How is you?

(Giselle walks in the door behind Jerry after a hard night at work.)

Giselle: Hello, Jerry and everybody. Lord, I am so tired. Mommy, where's Maria, like Jerry asked?

Studae: Sh-sh-sh-she's—

Grahams: Boy, please zip it. Giselle, your daughter was out last night drinking and … and … and—

Gisele (interrupting): Is my baby all right? Mommy, where's my baby? Lord, Lord, Lord!

Grahams: Baby, calm down. She's all right. She is asleep right now. Nothing happened to her, but she was crying drunk. That's how we found her in the backyard.

Giselle: Lord hold me back before I go off. What is her problem? Why is she so stupid, Lord? Let me have a seat.

Raul comes to the door and rings the bell. He is the town's drug pusher.

Raul: Good morning. How's everyone feeling? (No response.) Look, y'all, I am looking for Maria. Is she home? She left her purse in my car, and I wanted to return it before she panicked. Is she around?

Giselle: Boy, you bring my baby home drunk and crying, and now you want to see her again just a few minutes after picking with her head? Fool, are you crazy? You better not have given her any drugs.

Raul: Now hold on, Miss Lady. I did no such thing. I only hung out and had a few drinks. She's eighteen and can handle herself quite well, if I may add.

Giselle: Young man, first things first. I am not "Miss Lady." Address me as ma'am. And what the hell do you mean eighteen? My baby is sixteen. And she can handle herself quite well? What you are talking about? Did you do something to my girl? Did you? I will kill you if you touched my baby.

Raul: Miss, I mean ma'am, I didn't touch your daughter. She was in a fight with her girlfriend Shay, and Shay hit her head, but she's all right. I just wanted to be a gentleman and return her personal items. So thank you, and please continue to have a good morning.

Giselle: Whatever. Stroll on, Raul. Later. Bye-bye.

Raul goes out, slamming the door.

Jerry: Now can I go back and see my, I mean Maria? I am really concerned. Please, can I?

Grahams: No, baby. She might not be decent. Why don't you come back later and maybe then, okay, love? I will see you then.

Jerry: Okay, Ms. Grahams. I'll be back later, but please tell her not to leave. I will be back later. Bye-bye.

Later that evening, after everything has calmed down, the family waits for Maria to come out after her shower. There is a knock at the door, and it is Nicole, Maria's friend.

Nicole: Hello, Miss Giselle. Where is Maria? I want to talk to her. Is she all right?

Maria: Hello, girl. What's up? And why did you leave me last night—what up with that?

Nicole: No, love, you left me. Don't you remember? You got into the ride with Raul and wouldn't get out because you were sad that Shay hit her head.

Maria: No, no, chick. I remember that you started all that crap because she is dating your ex-boyfriend. Nicole, you need to let that go, girl. It's not right, and hell, he don't want you anymore.

Nicole: No, Maria. He will always want me, and I know that for a fact. Hell, he was at my house last night, and—well, that's between me and my man. Those two are history. And I mean history.

Maria: You're so wrong and a tramp, but hell, I like it. Way to get yours back. Handle up and get out. Bye-bye.

Nicole: Whatever. I will see you later. Bye, girl. Bye-bye Miss Giselle and Grahams.

Grahams (staring): Girl, you are out of your mind to fight your best friend over someone else's man. When are you going to learn that someone else's business is none of yours? You sit here cheering for a new friend that is wrong? You are all messed up. Lord, please help you. Be with her through this charade, Lord.

Giselle: I should slap you silly. What is wrong with you? haven't I been there for you? Where did I go wrong? Baby, what's wrong? (Starts to cry.) Baby, who introduced you to drinking?

Maria: Mommy, please don't cry. It's not your fault, it's all mine, and I will come around one day. But I am still young, so please don't worry too much for me. And Mommy, I taught myself to drink hanging out with my girl Lakeeba. As you can see, I can handle that also. Look at Uncle Tulip. He can drink and he stays clean while he does it. That's my uncle.

Giselle: Lakeeba, Li'l Sippy from around the way? I know she is from Mississippi, but to have a nickname like Li'l Sippy is a shame. Maria, baby, you're going to hurt yourself or end up in a bad situation if you don't slow down. Mark my words, baby; mark me down.

Jerry: Hello all once again. Hi, Maria. I heard you were down and out for a while. Is my— I mean, are you okay? Hey, did you hear that Lakeeba got arrested? Her family doesn't want to pay to get her out. She left the party the other night and got into a fight with Jo-Joan. Jo-Joan said Lakeeba was being disrespectful in asking her what was wrong with her at the club. Jo-Joan told her it was none of her business and called her a bitch. Lakeeba slapped Jo-Joan and told her to go die somewhere as she was only trying to help. Jo-Joan swung back and was stopped by the police, who seen Lakeeba throw the punch. Lakeeba was taken down and can't make bail. She is downtown as I speak.

Maria: Poor little Lakeeba. She is cool as a fan, Mom.

Giselle: Cool? She has you drinking now, and that is not cool, and she is not your friend, and I will not have it one bit. You hear me, young lady?

Jerry: They want to teach her a lesson. Maria, I really hate to see anything happen to my— I mean you. Are you sure you are all right? And someone needs to help Lakeeba before she ends up dead.

Maria: Jerry, boy, sit down and shut up. Shhh, be quiet before someone hears you. And yes, I am okay, but why have I not seen you for a few weeks? What's up with my friend? What's going on, man?

Jerry: Well, I have been staying away because I cannot take too much more of the abuse. Maria, look. I am in love with you and I cannot help it, so please don't be mad at me. I didn't want it to happen, but you are so lovely and so special, can I—

Maria (shocked): Now wait, Jerry; just wait. I don't see you like that, and I don't think I ever will. You're like my brother and we hang like girls. To tell you the truth, I thought in the back of my head that you were gay. I thought wrong.

Jerry: Gay? Please, girl. Never. I am not. I know who is, supposedly, but please don't worry about that one. It's kind of a hidden secret around here, if you know what I mean.

Maria: Boy, please do not hold info. What's up and who's out? Or should I say, who's in the closet? Come on, let me know.

Jerry: Well, love, I let you know how I feel, and you said no. I can live with that, but can we still be friends like before, please? And I can't say anything, because you know people talk. Too many ears.

Pep enters the house and looks at Jerry. At the same time, Studae comes into the house. Jerry, Pep, and Studae look each other down, remaining quiet.

Pep: Hello, everyone. What's up Jerry? Hello, Studae.

Jerry: Hello and good-bye, all. (Runs out.)

Studae: (stuttering) Boy, what's up? And you better not joke me and leave me alone anyway before I go off.

Pep: Whatever, fool. Get out of my way. At this point I don't care.

Mike, Pep's buddy, comes into the house.

Studae: Oh Lord, it's time to go. Don't you play with me also, Mikeeeeey.

Mike: Hello everyone. What's up, Pep? Why did you leave the party? I thought you were cool. What's wrong?

Pep: Man, come in the back room so we can talk.

May May comes into the room as Pep and Mike leave.

May May: Why is everyone staring at them two? Hello!

Giselle: Loud one, shut up and sit. Let's listen closely. Quiet, please.

May May: Okay, but why?

CHAPTER 5

SECRET

From the back room:

Mike: I love you, man, and I didn't take too kindly to see you push up on those fools. You're too cool for that crap.

The family is startled and remains quiet, because they don't really know what's up. They do, however, remember Jerry saying that someone was gay. But it couldn't be Pep and Mike. Damn! Pep and Mike come from the back room cool and head out the door, saying, "Later, everyone." The family truly understands that life is life, and no one should hate anyone because of status or preference in life.

Meanwhile Raul arrives outside and blows the car horn.

Maria: I am coming, Raul.

Gisele: Oh no, you're not, young lady. And I said that, not Grahams. Where do you think you're going, huh? Nowhere, young lady. Nowhere. Now take a seat.

Gisele opens the door and says good-bye to Raul.

Maria: Mom, why did you do that? There's a big party up the street, and Raul was giving me a lift. Man, I hate this place.

Grahams: Baby, don't talk back to your mother. Shush, girl. The Lord don't like ugly. Now go to your room.

Maria heads to her room but sneaks out of the back door, run toward Raul's car, and shouts for him to wait. Raul slows down. Maria jumps in the car, all smiles.

Raul: I thought you were a big girl. Now what's up with you and I tonight? Can we get our thing going?

Maria: We are going to get our party going and that's it, man. Let's go.

Raul: That's cool. You seem to be a big girl. You probably can handle a little pill, right, big girl?

Maria: I don't do drugs, fool. You're not going to push them on me. But I do drink, so what do you have in here, big boy?

Raul: I think we can get started with some Rémy Martin if you can hang, young lady.

Maria: I can hang. I will be hanging a lot when I am out of my Graham's home. I need to be free and explore the world like many others my age. I feel trapped sometimes in life. I feel that my life is being led by a plan my mother has for me, something other than what God has planned. I guess I can just smile and enjoy my time here with you, Raul. Although you are older, you are really hip to the young game. I think that is sexy in ya … (Laughs.)

Raul slips a couple of ecstasy pills in the bottle and pours Maria a drink. She drinks up and becomes dizzy and faints.t.

Raul: Yes; about time.

He drives off into the darkness.

CHAPTER 6

DEE DEE, TODD, AND RAUL

Operator: Collect call from Tin State Prison, will you accept the charges?

Dee Dee: Who could be calling me? It better not be Todd. I told this dude to leave it alone. But I better end this for good. Hell, it never got started. Yes, I will accept the charges.

Todd: Hi, baby. How you doing?

Dee Dee: I am doing fine, Todd, but what made you dial my number?

Todd: I was feeling lonely and abandoned by everyone and wanted to give you a call. I am to be released in a few and wanted to see what was up in your life.

Dee Dee: Well, Todd, my life is my life, and I am doing great. Look, why'd you really choose to call me? I mean, shouldn't you be calling your people or your girl who held you down for two years?

Todd: Nah, Dee Dee. I went in without a girl. Remember? I was trying to get at you, but you kept blocking me.

Dee Dee; I was blocking because I told you I am not into that life you love to live. I will never be. Like I said before, *we* will never be, so you have to let that thought go.

Todd: See, that is what I am talking about. I bet you still kicking it with Raul?

Dee Dee: Raul? Nah. Just like I told you, I told him. I am not into the life. Plus, I let it be known that I was not into grown-ass men. I wanted something in life, and I am on my way to getting it. So, if you will, please do me the honor of not calling me anymore. It is high enough, my cell phone bill, and now I have to pay for this call. Look, Todd, I wish you the best and truly hope you have changed, because I have in life.

Todd is livid at the thought of Raul still going after Dee Dee when it was known that Todd wanted her bad. Raul ignored Todd's plea to back away and let him get to know her. Raul killed any chance of Dee Dee and Todd when Raul mentioned how Todd was running hard and would end up in prison, which he eventually did three months later.

Todd also can't figure out how the cops had known his location and what he had stashed in his home. After the ass whipping Todd put on a customer, no one knew who had done it but one person. That person was Kyle, and he too would pay.

Raul didn't play games and didn't enhance Dee Dee's mind in any way. She still didn't want anything to do with any man involved in drugs.

Raul went about his business, Todd went to jail for two years, and Kyle kept on being an undercover snitch.

CHAPTER 7

SAVED BY THE BELL

As the car moves slowly into a dark parking lot, Raul is not at first aware that he is being followed from a distance by a blue sedan. He then sees the lights from the car and immediately adjusts his intention to attack Maria. Once the sedan pulls alongside, Raul sees the driver is Derek, with Pep in the passenger seat. They had been called to watch the house for Maria's departure.

Derek: So what's up, man? Why you are at the park? And what is wrong with my cousin, fool? I think you better think about what you are about to get into.

Raul (with a little smile): Man, I just thought she needed to get away and catch a little air, hombre.

Pep: Air, man? She looks like she needs a doctor. Fool, let my cousin out of that car before you get hurt, and I am not playing! (He touches his side.)

Maria is slurring and waking. She starts to question the scenery.

Maria: What's going on? Why am I here? Raul, what have you done to me? Where are we? Man, let me out of here. You're crazy. I don't believe it. I am so woozy. Did you slip me a trick? Oh God, did you? Oh, my head is spinning.

Raul: No, love. Nothing happened. I was only driving you up here to get a little air, that's all. Your cousins came by to check on the car. Right, fellas?

Derek: No, that's not right. I believe you were going to try a fast move that would have got you into a lot of trouble. I think it's time to go and maybe call the police. Come on, Maria; let's go home.

Raul: Man, no need for that. Maria is all right. Please take her home to relax. It's cool, right, everyone?

Maria: Since my cousin saved me, you had better start praying and hope to God that I don't want anyone else to know what you tried. I hate you, Raul. I really hate you.

Back at the family house, they await the arrival of Maria, who they discovered had left. But Giselle is not too sad, because Derek called and let her know he is on the tail.

Giselle: That damn girl just won't learn. Lord, please work with me. And yes, Lord, work with her.

Derek: All right folks, here she is. She is very upset, so please be patient with her.

Pep comes through the door, holding Maria up under her arms.

Giselle: Now what has happened, girl? Pep, Derek what happened? Oh, Lord.

Maria: Mom, I am okay. I just had a little something bad to drink.

Grahams: Girl, don't you stand there and lie to your own mother. What's become of you, and why did you leave after you were told to stay in the house? Why you are so hardheaded?

Giselle: Not hardheaded—stubborn, and just like your father

Maria: My father has nothing to do with this. Remember, he's not here. It's my entire fault, right? All mine. I didn't want to destroy what you two had. I was just a mistake, and you still take things out on me! (Crying.)

Giselle: Oh no, baby. I love you. I was the happiest person on earth when I learned that I was with child. I am still gloating at the thought of what we went through together as mother and child. Your father was just a sperm donor, not a father, and it had nothing to do with you, love.

Grahams: That's right, child. He was a good man at first. Then he got out in the world and started to drink and carry on like some kind of fool. The day he lifted his hand to my daughter was the day he had to go, or I would have struck him down! Lord help me.

Maria (crying): Can I please be excused? I am sorry. But I don't want to feel like I am living in a jailhouse or something. Remember, I am over sixteen. Oh man, I feel bad. Can we talk tomorrow?

As Maria heads to bed, Pep starts to tell where they found her, but is cut off by Derek. Derek says she was sitting at a restaurant with her girls, bent over in pain. Derek wants to protect her feelings from being embarrassed.

Tulip comes into the house.

Tulip: Man, weren't you two guys down at City Park an hour ago? I thought I saw your car, Derek, man. I guess you guys were out there getting a piece, huh, my man? Way to go and keep it up, boys. Where's the drink?

Giselle: Tulip, it's not the time to play. Please sit down and shut up. And seek help; you have a problem.

Tulip: The only problem I have is not getting enough juice in my system tonight before I turn in. Now what?

Tulip heads to the back room and goes to sleep.

Quotes of Life

Knowledge is not wasted if applied in life.

CHAPTER 8

TRULY CONCERN

Bootsie Jackie, who has a silent crush on Maria, enters the home. She is as mad as you know what.

BJ: No!… not my girl. Where are Maria's people? Where is my girl? I got a call from Patsy, who heard from James, who heard from Jo-Joan. That is my girl. Stop! Now where is Maria?

Giselle: Girl, sit down! And stop that noise right now. She is in her room.

BJ: Maria, girl, what in the world? You okay, girl? I heard what happened, and when I see that Raul, it's on. Messing with my girl like that. Man, I am so pissed. Who in the hell does he thinks he is?

Maria: Bootsie, Bootsie, Bootsie Jackie. Shut up! Damn, girl. You loud and my head hurt.

BJ: Oh, love, I am sorry, but can I at least hold you? I need a hug after all of this.

Maria: Look, Bootsie, I may be dizzy, but I ain't crazy. I know what you have been feeling in the back of your head for me, and let me tell you: it ain't gone happen. I like boys, boys, and boys.

So please step back and, hell, leave me alone right now. Go, girl, and come back tomorrow. I need to sleep.

BJ: Oh. Okay, I see. You've known this long and didn't say anything. I thought you were feeling me, girl. Now I see you were playing our friendship. Okay. Okay. Okay, I see.

Maria: Girl, shut up. You knew I was aware of what was going on. My girls knew what you were up to and joked me a few times. But I am not that way, Bootsie Jackie, and I am sorry. All that I can say is I do love you. Now please come and hug me … and then go home!

The girls hug. Bootsie Jackie is okay with Maria's decision. She leaves and heads home, happy with the minor conversation with Maria, knowing that they can only and will only be friends.

BJ: Bye, everyone. Talk to you later.

Gisele: Bye, baby. (Whispering:) That child, that child. Lord, help her find her identity.

Rolanda comes through the door, having been called by Gisele about Pep's issue.

Rolanda: Pep, come here, li'l boy.

Pep: Mom, I am not a li'l boy.

Rolanda: Pep, don't sass me. You're my li'l boy now and forever. I am your mother. Now what in the world have you been doing?

Pep: Nothing, Mommy. I only had a few with Uncle Tulip a few times. I am okay.

Rolanda looks at Tulip, her brother, and is about to go off when she is interrupted by Giselle.

Giselle: You drunk fool, giving youngsters alcohol. What is your problem, man? I ought to slap you sober!

Rolanda: Nah, not you ought to; I am about to do it. Come here, Tulip!

Grahams: All right now. Everyone sit down!

Rolanda: Mom, your ignorant son has been feeding my boy alcohol.

Tulip: Slow down all you, slow down. Yes, so what? I gave him a little sip to ensure he stays away. He always inquires about it and why I drink so much. He said it must taste like Kool-Aid, the way I been sipping all my life.

Rolanda: But Tulip, you knew that was not right. That is my baby, my only child. (Crying:) Lord, what were you thinking?

Giselle: Momma, I know you said to sit down, but I just have to touch him. Please, Lord, allow me to lay my hands on him, touch him, and bring him back to the living. *Because his behind is already dead*!

Rolanda: Tulip, I am ashamed of you. After his father died, you were supposed to be one of his guides in life, not his death.

Tulip: Everyone, I am sorry for my actions. I was wrong, I was wrong, and Pep ... I am sorry. Please forgive me for my stupidity. I meant you no harm. I was only trying to damage your taste buds for alcohol. I will never do it again to anyone. I am sorry. (Walks away with tears in his eyes.)

Pep: Uncle Tulip, I knew what you were doing. I wanted to try it to ensure it wasn't for me. And Uncle Tulip, it is not. I am not the one.

Derek: Way to go, cuzz. Way to go.

Rolanda: Way not to go. Get home now. You're punished, son, and I mean punished. Don't think about any party. Tulip, we will talk soon, but for now I accept your apology. Don't let it happen again, you hear me, boy?

Tulip: Yes, my dear sister ... I hear you.

Grahams grabs her handbag and heads to the door. She tells them that she is going to the store, but really she is heading to the city jail to see Lakeeba, Maria's friend.

At the jail:

Grahams: Good day. I would like to see a Lakeeba Johnson.

In the visiting room, she awaits Lakeeba, who is escorted by a counselor, Devin.

Devin: Good day, ma'am. Are you her guardian?

Grahams: No, sir, I am not. I am her savior.

Devin: Ma'am, what are you saying?

Grahams: I am here to take her home and deliver her from this pain.

Devin: Ma'am, we can only get her released if you are her guardian. That is why I escorted her to you—to set up AA counseling.

Grahams: Then that is who I am, her guardian. Can I please take my child home?

Devin: We can start the release paperwork in a moment, but first we will need to know where she will reside. She has been living from hand to hand and used by many who wish her no good in life.

Grahams gives her address. They are taken to a room to discuss the parameters of Lakeeba's release back into civilization. Of course Lakeeba is crying and ashamed of her life, but welcomes a change from a woman with one of the biggest hearts in America …

The next day, as everything returns to normal, Cheyenne comes over with someone who wishes to speak to Maria about Maria's fight with Shay.

Cheyenne: Hello, family. How's it going, and where is Maria?

Giselle: After you two had that argument the other night, you want to speak to her? Good move on your part.

Maria: Hello, Cheyenne. What's up?

Cheyenne: Well, I was sitting on my porch, and I kept seeing this green car pass by. I was getting worried. Guess who it was that kept driving by? Well, stop guessing—it was Shay. She expressed her concerns and wanted to talk to you, but didn't know how to approach.

Maria: I was wanting to talk to her. Where is she?

Shay comes into the house when she hears Maria ask for her.

Shay: Good morning, everyone. Hello, Maria. I was really wanting to talk to you about the other night.

Maria: Look, Shay, as I lay across the bed last night, I was seriously thinking of you and wondering how I should come to you and apologize for my actions. I am sorry. I was only thinking of myself and not our friendship. I should have taken Nicole's word over yours.

Shay: That's why I was so upset. We have been girls for so long, and I really felt that you let me down by not allowing me to express myself. But maybe I was being too forward, and I am sorry for that. And I love you.

Maria: Can I have a hug, please? And to let you know, your man and Nicole are "back together," as she puts it.

Shay: Really? She can have him. I was only using him to get what I could. But if she wants to get played by a no-good guy … Good luck. I am happy.

Cheyenne: Can I have a hug? Because you went off on me also, girls, and I was just trying to hang out with you.

Maria: Come here, girl. You know I love you.

Giselle: Love is love. And you're punished, Maria, for two weeks.

Maria: Mom! Why, I was only trying to show the girls that I can, I can … Umm … Umm … Mom, please.

Grahams (laughing): Well, love, I guess they know now.

Maria: But Mom, Granny, there is a big party next week, and I was going with Derek and Pep. Also, Jesus was going with his girl. The whole family is going to be there, but not me.

Mom, please let me off for the weekend. I will do another week of punishment. Can I please go, Mom? Please?

Giselle: Well, Maria, it depends on how well you carry yourself this week.

Maria: All right, Mom. Thank you. I won't let you down this time; I won't.

Grahams: Don't be good, stay good. Lord help me.

Studae (stuttering): Man, I have never seen such love and emotion from a family.

Everybody: Studae, shut up!

Grahams starts to cry when she sees Lakeeba come from her room. Lakeeba slept with Grahams all night and cried in her arms until she fell asleep.

CHAPTER 9

OMG!

Bootsie Jackie has left Maria's home and heads to her spot.

Shay: Oh, shit, you scared me. What the hell you doing here? I thought you wanted nothing to do with me since you are on a straight and narrow now in life. I am on a need to have right now. I need to get mine, and I thought you were hungry and needed a bite. But if you choose to let it walk away, then so be it.

BJ: Now hold on. I am never one to turn down good grub, and I won't at this point. I just don't get you and the way you play me and all. You know I am not for the bullshit you play. I need a trick that is down for me and not a momentary love.

Shay: I can only be a moment because I have plans in life, and they don't include being a lesbian. I just enjoy your company, and I have needs that are not being met. Shit, I am greedy—so what? If I am, then it is your job to feed me, or should I say feed you.

BJ: Shay, you know it is always about you. I can't get a snack unless it is about you. I wake up and you call, I go to sleep and you call. I go out with another chick and there you go, showing up out of nowhere. I need for you to respect my space and stop being so jealous. This is not about you and me. It is about you and you. I can't commit to you in any way. I can commit to myself that it ain't about you. Now if I am wrong, let me know, but if I am not, then you can just know that I am being me and staying away from you. But truly what is wrong with you?

Shay: There is nothing wrong with me other than being in love. I do love you, BJ, but you choose to just walk on like you don't know it.

BJ: Shay, I know. I just want you to slow down and recognize my space. I got you, but we have a secret relationship. You don't want it out, but yet you act as if we are out there. Make up your mind. Hell, I need to make up mine before I am completely lost in this game.

Shay: What do you mean, completely lost? You having doubts about your sexuality?

BJ: Now there you go, tripping, always tripping ... Look, Shay, you and I know we have nothing here. I am trying to make a move on your girl. So why play with me and my attempt to concur? You know you ain't right, girl. In fact you are foul, and I think I am not interested in eating anything tonight. So bounce, chick.

Shay: Nah, chick. It ain't like that at all. I came here for a purpose, and it will happen or I will beat your hard ass. So trip if you want, but we getting it on and you will serve me right. Now make a move and open the door, BJ. Do it now.

BJ: Okay, since you put in like that. Bring your ass on in here. And you better not run because it is on …

CHAPTER 10

THREE HOURS LATER

J-Cob and his boys Tricky Tee and Kyle are driving the streets. They spot Shay leaving BJ's home.

Tee: WTF! I knew she was hiding something because I tried my best to get in that.

J-Cob: Man, I guess she didn't want you and your tricks, fool. She wanted what she is getting from the dude chick … a tongue. (Laughs.)

Tee: Yeah, you might be right. But what if they were just talking and hanging out, man?

J-Cob: Nah. They are at it because BJ don't play. When she wants something, she gets it. If they go inside her crib, I heard it is on and all hell breaks loose, with screaming and all types of freaky shit a girl/dude can do to a woman.

Tee: I can only say, if she likes it, I love it. I just know she has some good shit, dog, because it is not being hit right.

It is being abused by a woman who wants to be a man. (Laughs.)

Shay walks to her mother's SUV. Her phone rings.

Shay: Hello? Oh, hi, Nicole, how are you?

Nicole: I am okay. I just want to apologize and let you know that I am so sorry. You good, girl. But I have been calling you for over two hours. I thought something was wrong.

Shay: Nah. I am good but a little sore. I hurt my leg, but I will be okay. Hey, let me hit you tomorrow. I have a call coming in …

Nicole: Cool, later.

For Shay, driving is painful. She is still coming from the thrill/pain ride of her life. She basically fell out after BJ did unthinkable things to her, leaving her with a smile. Her cell phone rang until she turned it off. They hugged and slept.

Kyle and Tricky Tee are smoking weed as J-Cob drives. Kyle is starting to hog the weed and not pass the product. He is holding on for dear life to the drug. He truly wants the more powerful hit of crack. Tricky Tee and J-Cob have been helping to wean Kyle off the crack, but the pressure of needing that rush is starting to play its part. They are finding it harder and harder to hold him down.

Kyle was born a crack baby to a mother who lived the street life. No matter how her family tried to pull her back, it panned out that she died while giving birth. Kyle was left to suffer alone and come up in a foster home.

Kyle, although a funny guy and one to bring all to laughter, is really strung out bad. He is only a few hits from joining his mother. On top of that, Kyle is a gossiper and speaks the truth as a way of supplying himself with the drug he needs to survive.

Tricky Tee, of course, is a sore loser, only looking for his next victim in life, and soon to find it behind bars in a jail cell.

Tricky Tee is the cousin of Shay. He is not one to keep secrets. But for one startling piece of information, it may be right to keep his mouth closed. His thirst for money and drugs will play a vital part in his ability to remain quiet.

Tricky Tee moved to town with his aunt, Ms. Carroll. She basically threw him in the streets when he challenged her and said he didn't need her or their sorry-ass family.

It happened on a Saturday. Tee and Kyle were sitting on the porch, talking about getting high and watching a game, with a couple of girls working their magic at halftime. But that was not to be. Ms. Carroll intended to travel out of town, leaving the house for Tee to take care of. Just an hour before she was to leave, she heard Thaddeus Wilson—or as his street name had it, Tricky Tee—planning a getup at her blessed home.

Tee spat off at the mouth, not realizing that he had it good. Ms. Carroll placed a call to his mother to inform her of her disappointment with Tee. Her sister simply said, "I told you so, Carroll."

The pain was laid out in pure fashion. There Carroll was, stuck with her foot in her mouth, but not for long. She had a plan for any and all who crossed her path. Grahams was to play a vital role in the setup.

Tee meanwhile has to fend for himself and do him any way he can. But what is he to do about Shay and her antics in life? He knows that he has an up on Shay, but with her mother, Ms. Carroll, now mad at him, how is she going to take the news about Shay being on both side of the street—bisexual? Although he is an undercover thug hanging in the streets, he still is a softy for his aunt and her generosity. She took him in like a son and a protector of the family. Now he stands alone with a loaded weapon to use at any moment. Blackmail can be his lift.

Tee's phone rings. It is Shay.

Shay: What up, cuzz? Where you at? Or should I say, where you guys going, because I seen you drive past Bootsie Jackie's crib.

Tee: Yeah, yeah, Shay, that was up. But what you doing out this way? You got a dude up in these parts? (Giggles.) I mean, why you on the side of town, chick?

Shay: Boy, don't play. I know you're tripping and seen me leave Bootsie's crib. That is cool. I know what you are thinking, and it ain't that type of party, dude. Not at all. She is my friend, and I chill now and then with her. Ain't no thing. So don't get it twisted, Tee. And tell ya boys I got that laughing I hear in the background. I am strictly. Ya heard me. Strictly.

Shay is scared about being caught leaving Bootsie Jackie's crib. What is she to do, tell the truth and be laughed at by her girls? Nah. She lied.

She ends the call and tells Tee she is headed home and will see him there. Tee won't be there, but he simply says, "'Ight."

Shay then calls Bootsie Jackie to let her know the deal. Bootsie laughs and tells Shay to shut up and not worry. BJ is cool and doesn't blab her business. As Shay stated, they're friends and chill now and then.

Bootsie is tired and quickly ends the phone call. She lies down with a smile on her face, planning her next move to get at Maria …

CHAPTER 11

MORE ISSUES

May May heads to Ms. Carroll's after Carroll called to talk of her pain in kicking out Tee.

May May: Hey girl, what's up?

Carroll: Not much but this nephew of mine. Here I am, trying to do the right thing for him, and he goes out here and plots a party for him and his no-good boy Kyle with his strange behind. I mean, every time I see him, his eyes are red and he looks sleepy. It creeps me out. How can Tee want to plan a striptease act with girls and his behind?

May May: Because he always has money from stealing and selling the drugs he uses, from what I heard.

Carroll: Now how do you know all this?

May May: Because I hear things, and you know they can't keep secrets in the church. Ya know his father is really trying to reach him, but Tee has nothing to say to his father. He has always steered far away from him once he found out that man was his dad.

Carroll: As for Kyle, he needs the Lord.

May May: And not any more drugs. The more he plays around with that crap, the more he drifts into the land of no coming back and eventually death.

Carroll: Please don't say that. There is a way, and one day the light will shine bright. The Lord has not called his name for a reason.

May May: Not at the moment, but it is so close. Have you seen him lately? All skinny and pale. How can anyone puff-puff pass a joint or anything with him? So sad, and almost too late.

Carroll: I know, girl. But back to Tee and his antics: it is a shame before God that he has not one ounce of forgiveness in him for his father.

May May; How can he after what every woman has been through who has come into contact with that man? His dad has no respect for women at all. He was and probably is still all about getting his in life and nothing else. He has probably fathered more kids out there and abandoned them as well. And now he wants to find his way?

Carroll: I just don't get these newfound Christians who live foul lives, and when age catches up, they find peace in their wrongdoings. I guess everyone screws up in life, trying to avoid the devil that causes so much pain.

May May: Pain shouldn't have to be felt so deep to get a point across. There have been so many who have suffered such painful situations and have lived great lives. That is what I don't get when it comes to our faith. I mean, a preacher will sit up there and preach about how the Lord wants us all to suffer in life to gain more appreciation for our sins. The Lord wants us to repent, ask for forgiveness, and pray for his holy hands. So many hands have reached up with bloodstains thick as wet sand, only to suffer more in life. It has gotten out of hand in many ways. The more we look for a way, the more we are let down and placed in the rotten holes many of us have climbed out of in the past.

Carroll: May May, I know, girl. I have thought the same many times in life. But the faith I have been brought up with convinces me to smile and shine. I know there is light at the end of the tunnel for my sister and brothers and me. If you believe, you will be blessed.

May May: Carroll, I believe, but must I be permitted into the gates of heaven with a stained memory of pain? I mean, how someone can forget what they have endured in life to walk a clear, crystal path to heaven? I find myself doubting if there is such a place. All we see are the symbols of the dead and the sinful ones, and not the light. Take a look in this world today. It is evident that we are all cursed in some way. Africa's suffering, many foreign countries' suffering, and it seems not to have an end. Wars and false victories proclaimed by our former president. People shooting each other and the people in office. For what? I just don't get this crap.

Carroll: I know. Those poor souls in Texas and their family members who fought the false war, only to be gunned down by one of their own soldiers ... OMG! The list grows, girl, and all for what? Our economy is at a standstill because the rich want the seat of the presidency and will do whatever to get it, even if it's the starvation of their countrymen, and that is so sad. Every month a fight goes on in DC over the haves and have-nots. It has become a simple headache. I find myself not wanting to watch the news because they will cloud it up all day with a recent incident or talk about the fight in DC.

May May: Yeah, girl. Even the local news reports nothing but out-of-town news and leaves the suffering alone, as it is not important.

Carroll: Yeah. They will report a child kidnapped from another city but won't report about a child from their own city. And let's not talk about the race of many who clog the news. Now and then one minority face may appear. The world is so confused. What can you do but pray?

May May (laughing): But girl, when Tee and Kyle slow down, the earth will shake. It will be worth the wait, and all know that it will be a blessing. But girl, speaking of gossip, I was over at Graham's, and I heard Maria on the phone with Jo-Joan. She said something of Jo-Joan being upset and crying.

Carroll: Girl, these confused people of today don't know which way to turn. It is all about the bull these days and not the horse. (Laughs.) Everyone wants their say in life and not life. I can't understand. I just can't. I heard Maria when she said that Jo-Joan was clubbing and saw Tee, Kyle, and Paul's brother J-Cob. J-Cob was having words with a girl. Anyway, I was like, "Dang, Grahams, be quiet so I can hear!" Grahams told me to steer clear of the kids' business and all will work out. But you know me; I am nosey for a reason. (Laughs.)

CHAPTER 12

MARIA

Maria, feeling better, enters the kitchen with a big smile.

Maria: What in the world? Why is the place so somber? I am okay, good people, and ready to live. I apologize for being stupid, but I am young, right?

Grahams: Child, sit and eat and shut up before I bless you with my hands. (Smiling.) Now, what will my baby have for breakfast? I love you, child. Of course you know that?

Maria: Yes, Granny …

Maria's phone rings.

Maria: Excuse me for a minute. That's my cell ringing in my room. It must be important. Who could this be?

She retrieves the phone.

Maria: Hello? 'Ight. I will try. Stay cool, girl. I got you.

Returning to the kitchen, Maria laughs and eats breakfast with her family, but with a heavy mind. After breakfast, Maria showers and heads to the porch to await her friend Shay.

Maria: Shay! What up, girl? What is wrong now? You sounded so upset.

Shay: Yeah, girl, um, look. I want to be frank with this, but you have got to keep this to yourself.

Bootsie Jackie knows things in life, and being gay, she hears and sees a lot. What she seen lately is a trip to me and many.

Maria: And how do you know these things? You seem to know a lot of things lately, especially when it comes to Bootsie Jackie.

Shay: Girl, I am trying to open up and tell you things. Hell, I need to confide in someone because this is eating me up … Look, Maria, Bootsie told me last night that J-Cob is down low.

Maria: What?

Shay: Yeah, girl, and he's been trying to cover it up for a while. BJ said that she saw J-Cob hugging Jo-Joan last week, and now he's all up in Lakeeba's face trying to holla. But I seen Lakeeba slap him as she was leaving the club. BJ had business to attend to in life. I want you to hold your comments, Maria …

Marie: How can I sit still when you have hit me in the head? Oh my God! What will Paul say?

Shay: He won't say anything because he already knows. That is why you never see them together. Paul and his father are embarrassed. J-Cob thinks they don't know, but the way they treat Jo-Joan when the see her … him … I mean Jo-Joan—it's a shame.

Maria: I am lost for words, girl. I think someone is going to get hurt. Someone already is hurting. And it is Jo-Joan. Girl, that fool is in love with J-Cob and won't let it go. Shim stalks him all the time. J-Cob cares for shim also but won't admit it at all, trying to play hard for his boys. But his father, Mr. Chad … I wonder how he is really taking it. You seem to know a lot. Why would BJ confide in you? Tell me that, girl.

Shay: Well, because I have been sleeping with Bootsie Jackie.

Maria: What?

Shay: Yes, but I don't feel gay. I just need to get mine, and that is it. I love men, but that girl knows how to put it down. She leaves me shaking and in anticipation for the next time I let her have me.

Maria: Let her have you? Shay, are you crazy? Girl, all this time and I never knew you were a lesbian … OMG!

Shay: Well, I'd rather be a lesbo than down low, because men want a woman who is open. Women don't want men who have been opened. (Laughs.)

Maria: Girl, you are nasty. Ugh! How could you do things like that?

May May is sitting in the window, listening with her mouth open. She loves to gossip …

Shay: I just wanted you to know because BJ is really after you. She only serves me to keep her time busy and satisfy her urges until she can get her claws in you. But Maria, I tell you that because I want you to not give in to her. I want her to find herself. I will be friends with her, but that is it, or at least until I find a man to hold me down.

Maria: Like I said, ugh! Shay, you are a trip. BJ will never, and I mean never, have a moment with me like that. It is all about a man when it comes to me. My family didn't raise me to munch on carpet. I was raised to walk like a lady and be served like a lady. So you and BJ can have a great time relaxing and … whatever you do. (Laughs.)

Shay: It is all good. I just wanted to be open and confide in you. You don't need to hold it against me.

Maria: I am and I will. I need for you to come back to your side and wait until your man comes along, girl. Please think of what you are doing. If it is right or not, I don't care. I just want my girl to be a girl and date a boy. Damn! (Crying.) You wrong, Shay.

Shay: You are wrong. I know I am, but please know I am stopping today. BJ hurt me bad last night, like I did her something wrong. I can't sit still at all. I am never letting her at me again. But I want you to really not give in to her or she will hurt you. She acts like she is mad at the women of this world, and that is why she is who she is in life.

Maria: Okay, girl. I got you. But Shay, please stay away until we find out what is wrong and if BJ needs some help. I don't want her to send you to a hospital. How could you explain that?

Shay: I do want you happy, Maria.

Maria: And I want you happy too, Shay …

Quotes of Life

When you have lost the consciousness of respect for our ancestors, you have lost in life.

CHAPTER 13

THE CRISIS

BJ (crying): Why me? Why me? Look at me. A damn man I want to be, when I am not. Why me? Lord, you tell people that you will be there for them, but you are not me. You have failed and failed me. You let me get abused by men and by women. You let my mother put me out there for what? A few measly dollars. You said to live for you and you would protect me. Lord, I am the one that you promised to help. I prayed to you. I reached for help. I cried out to you, but you didn't answer me. What did I do to deserve to be used and not wanted in life? I never hurt a soul. I went to school, respected my parents, and loved all I came in contact with, but no. I had to be abused and used and kicked out in the streets to create this identity of wanting to be a man.

All I want to do is hurt others who seem happy. I want to hurt someone who has not done anything but who has what I didn't, and that is a family. A loving grandmother, a mother who cares. I want Maria to pay for my pain. I need for her to pay for my pain. She is what I want to be, and that is loved. Lord, you let me down. I will get my revenge on those who hurt me. One by one, they all will pay—believe me in that. But I will start with Maria. I have done with Shay over and over, but her crazy ass keeps coming back for more. Frankly, I am tired of her.

My mother the whore will pay. The men of my family will pay. That drug Lord surely will pay if I have my say-so. I can't forget and I won't forgive. I have been scared, and for what? An orgasm I didn't understand.

It ain't over, God. It ain't over. And I tell you what else. I am not gay or a lesbian. I am a woman who wants to get out and be loved by a man. I can't because I am afraid to be hurt and dogged again in life. So I pretend to like girls when I don't. I just want to inflict pain on any and whomever in life. Basically, I don't care. And I won't, Lord.

You said it would be okay, you had my back, you love me, you care for me, and you would protect me. (Screams:) *From what*? Blood is my only salvation, and I shall have it one way or the other. That you can believe.

Her cell phone rings …

CHAPTER 14

PAUL

Paul: J-Cob, man, I need to talk to you, and it can't wait.

J-Cob: What up, dude? Why are you tripping?

Paul: Nah, man. You tripping. You living a lie, dude.

J-Cob (nervously): What you talking, dude?

Paul: I am talking your bullshit, J-Cob, and you hurting someone in the process.

J-Cob: Hurt who, man?

Paul: Woman, dog!

J-Cob: What? Man, stop tripping. There is plenty in the streets other than Maria. Don't worry; I can't have them all. (Laughs.)

Paul: Man, this is not a joke. I am talking about the lie that you live.

J-Cob: What? (Starts to shake.)

Paul: Yeah, dude, I know. And you knew for a long time that I was on to you. How in the world did you fall into that world, dude? I mean, my brother, a queer. Who would have thought the big bad gang member is a faggot?

J-Cob rushes Paul and they start to fight. Chad enters from his room. He has been listening the entire time.

Chad: *Stop*! I said stop now, you two. (Pulls them apart) I am so hurt to have you two fighting. More than that, I hear from my room that you, J-Cob are gay. Is this true?

J-Cob: Yes, sir, it is true. It started when I was in jail. I can't help it. I am in love with another guy.

Chad slaps the hell out of J-Cob. J-Cob falls to the floor. He looks up, angry and ready to attack, but notices Paul is ready to defend their father.

Chad: Now son, I asked a question, and I didn't need a smart-ass response. I told you never to raise your voice, but you did in an attempt to prove what, young man? What? That you are gay in life and want the comfort of another man. I didn't raise you like this, Jacob. I raised you hard and to always be in control. But no, you want to go out and embarrass me like this.

J-Cob: Pop, what you mean embarrass you? It has always been about you and what you wanted and never about us boys. You were the mean one, with the respect all around town, but Mom suffered in her own way with you. You and you only wanted what was best for you. I love you, Pop, but I have the right to live my life and not yours, Mr. Chad the powerful one.

Paul: Watch your mouth, boy, before I wear your behind out. You heard me?

J-Cob: Yeah, Paul, I hear you. You have always been Pop's favorite, never in trouble and not sent to jail like I was. But my big Pop couldn't stop that, right, Pop? I was sent to prove a point about your kid surviving in prison. Yeah, Pop, I survived. And because of your reputation, I was raped in prison on the third day as I walked to chow. All the while I was being attacked, they repeated your name because you hurt someone in their family years ago. I had nothing to do with that. So I became a prag and lived under cover in prison, all while sending you powerful letters, fake letters. But I vowed to kill every one of those who attacked me and made me live foul. Then I met this wise guy who had respect, and he told them to leave me alone. I became his lover in prison. He was sentenced to life, and all he knew was jail, but he took care of me and showed me the way. I grew to love him. Then it came time for my release. The day I left prison, he killed himself because he couldn't survive in there without me. So I came home damaged goods and living a lie. I met Jo-Joan and we hit it off. He promised to keep my secret, but I see he has not.

Paul: Nah. He has kept the secret, so don't be mad at your faggot lover. Be mad that I followed you to a hotel outside of town and waited almost three hours as you and he did whatever you do to each other. You make me sick, li'l brother. I mean sick.

Chad; Now Paul, that is your brother. He don't deserve this. He deserves love and support on any level, and we will give it to him. I caused him to be damaged, and I will live up to helping him in life, no matter what, even if this life is the one he chose to live. Although I don't agree, I will accept you for whoever you are in life. I just ask, as your brother stated earlier, that you leave women alone if this is your life. There is too much out there. I don't need people's lives played with, whether it be physical or emotional. Do you hear me, young man?

J-Cob: Yes, sir, I do. I want to make you proud, Dad; I do. But how can I when I live a lie? I will be a man and survive, Pop. I just need help in becoming who I am in life. I have my father who understands me, Paul. (Rises from the floor.) Look, I am sorry, big brother. I didn't want to hurt you or cause any problems for the family, but I am who I am in life. I know I didn't start this way. You were always there for me. But I was taken away and introduced to a life I like and I identify with. I was not born this way, but this is who I have become, and I must be honest to the world and myself. I have to live my life happy or end up taking it, as many have who feel the pressure of life and the pain of a family member not wanting them for who they are. I am sorry Paul. I am.

Paul rushes over. He grabs and hugs J-Cob.

Paul: No need, little brother. I love you and I am sorry, J-Cob. I am truly sorry for my actions. I was just so pissed because you didn't tell me. I had to find out on my own.

J-Cob: You mean no one else knows?

Paul: I am quite sure some people know. But you have to do what is right. I hate to say this, but Jo-Joan is on the brink of hurting him/herself. Jo-Joan was confiding in Maria about the hurt that he endured watching you kissing some girl in the club.

Chad: See, son? There you go, already doing what I asked you not to do in life. What of this girl you kissed? These down-low people really piss us true men off. I want you to stop. I mean it, now. Stop!

J-Cob: Pop, I am sorry to tell you that was a front. I am not interested in that girl. I seen Jo-Joan come in the club, and I didn't want him to put our business out. So I was talking to this girl I met a few times in the club. She likes to come in and dance, but she is distant in many ways, like she is running and always on the move. I got slapped for that move and she stormed off. Pop, it was just a simple peck on the lips, but it worked. Jo-Joan left the club in a hurry, and I held on to my secret for one more day. I am sorry. But get this, Pop: my boy Tricky Tee said ugh because he always says that girl could pass for my sister. To be frank, she does look like us in a way.

Chad: What did you say, son?

J-Cob: I said—

Chad: I know what you said, and what club—better yet, where does she live, son?

J-Cob: I don't know. Why all the questions?

Paul: Yeah, Pop. What is going on here?

Chad: That girl you kissed could be your sister.

Paul/J-Cob (together): *What*?

Chad tells the boys of his life before their mother. He leaves them in disbelief and goes in search of their sister, who is a runaway from a home in Mississippi.

No More Wrongdoing

Please, my brother, no more
We've been through so much already.
No more. We've lost and it cost
You and me; our people have lost so much.
I mean, look at community.
Just look: shacks for homes
Trash in streets to walk over
Rinky-dink corner stores to buy food
Wine and winos. Pimps, pushers
The smell, and we can't forget the jailhouses
Located throughout our neighborhoods.
No more, please; no more wrongdoing.
Back in the day, our leaders said from day one
Times will change, hang in there, hang in there.
And we did; yes, I know that we have.
But throughout it all there's still no jobs
And we still are not getting the proper nourishment.
But tell me, my brother—does our food
need to come from one's blood?
Blood that stains your hands for your entire life
Hands of king and queens.
My brother, no more. Instead of guns
Think about what you're doing.
My brother, you helped build this
nation: houses and buildings
Cars, trucks, factories, airplanes, and ships, my brother.
You created medicine, food, music, and poetry
Colleges and universities and so much more.

You've created children, and you too,
my brother, were that child.
No more, no more, no more wrongdoing.

So what do I do, you ask?
Take what you can the right way
And in the end it'll be okay.
No more, no more, no more …

CHAPTER 15

THE TURNAROUND/BIG BO

Lakeeba: Good morning, everyone.

Maria: Lakeeba! Girl, what you doing here, and coming from my granny's room? What is going on here?

Grahams: Lakeeba will be staying with us for a little while. She is now a resident of our home.

Giselle, Maria, Shay, Nicole, and Studae, stuttering: *What*?

Grahams: I am now her legal guardian. I want you all to open the arms God gave you and welcome her to our home.

The girls immediately run to Lakeeba and embrace her. Giselle stands by in dismay.

Giselle: Wait! Wait! Wait! Now, are you the young lady that introduced my baby to alcohol?

Lakeeba (in her country accent): Yes, ma'am, and I am so sorry. I wanted a friend to help me feel good about what

I was doing, and I dragged her into my life. But she said she already had a drink before I gave her some.

Giselle: Baby, how old are you and where's your mother?

Lakeeba: Ma'am, I am seventeen years old, and I ran away from a no-good person. I needed help and protection that my mother couldn't give me. I found it in a bootleg to block out my pain.

Giselle: Ah, baby, I am so sorry. But alcohol is not the answer. Is your failure to advance in life?

Lakeeba: Ma'am, you don't know how it is to lock your bedroom door every night so you won't be violated. I mean, (crying) he would come into my room and touch me in places I never touch. He would kiss on me and hold me down and then force himself on me. I was only a little girl, ma'am. Only a little girl. I told my mother and I cried and cried, only to be told to stop lying.

Giselle: Oh, child, I am so sorry. But you are going to be all right. God has got control now.

Lakeeba: She accused me of trying to break up her happiness. Ma'am, all I wanted was my momma! That is all. My momma! (Crying.) She told me I was the cause of her unhappiness with men. And no one wanted her because of me, and if her man touched me, I asked for it to get back at her mistreatment of me. (Cried so hard she is screaming.)

Grahams: Okay, baby. I got you now. You will be okay. Come here, baby; come here …

The room remains silent for a few minutes as all present wipe flowing tears. They feel Lakeeba's pain, and all are upset with her mother.

Maria has maintained her personal promise to herself and her family to behave. Her mom has agreed to let her go to the party with her family members, to return no later than midnight. But as always, Maria has other plans, and they don't include listening to anyone at any time.

The turnaround is set up by Mia-Duke. She has been hanging on the phone for a couple of days and really wants her family back, for love is within her heart.

Grahams: Baby, I know we did the right thing in letting Maria go with her family tonight. My Lord has plans. Yes, my Lord has plans, and I know this.

May May: What is wrong with Momma, Giselle?

Giselle: I don't know. She has just been singing all day and hanging around that phone a lot, talking about her Lord's plans.

May May: I wonder who she has been talking to and about what?

Giselle: I think something about a family gathering.

Cousin Big Bo bursts through the door to visit the family.

Big Bo: Grahams, what's up, baby? How's my favorite aunt doing? Girl, you're looking good.

Grahams: Boy, shut up but don't stop. And Big Bo, I am so glad to see you made it. Now let me talk to you later about you know what.

Gisele: Cousin Big Bo, looking good and free, let me stop before I commit a crime. Boy, where's your momma?

May May: Now girl, leave that man alone. Baby, what's going on with your mom?

Big Bo: She's all right, May May.

Cheyenne: Uncle Big Bo, Uncle Big Bo, how are you doing?

Big Bo: Girl-girl, how you are doing? You're looking more and more like May May.

Cheyenne: Tripping as usual again, right? No, I don't look like Mrs. May.

Big Bo: May May, still have not opened up as I see.

Giselle: Don't start, Big Bo. The Lord knows the time.

Big Bo: I hear the Lord speaking. Miss knows it all.

May May: Please, Big Bo, don't spoil happy times.

Cheyenne: You older people trip out too much for me. I am out of here.

May May: You're right, Big Bo. (Crying.) Cheyenne, we have to talk. Please don't leave. It's very important. Please wait. My sweet family, my husband and I have not been fighting. We have been talking a long time about this date, and I guess he was right in saying it has arrived. We never fight; we plan every three months for me to come out and visit, to see my baby face-to-face.

Giselle: Oh, I love you, girl. I am so sorry for interfering in your plans. Please, love, continue on with what you're saying.

May May: I love you, Giselle, and I was not mad at you. I knew why you were always upset with me. It's because of my past. I love you, sis, but let me continue and we will talk later.

Cheyenne: What's going on in here, people? Something just ain't right; I can feel it. Tell me something, please.

Grahams: The truth …

Big Bo: everything is all right, baby. Please just sit down. Come on, now. Just calm down, okay, love? Come on, everyone. It's time to go to another room.

Cheyenne: Somebody please talk to me. Is my mom all right? I'm going home now!

May May: Nah, love, your mom is fine. In fact, baby, your moms are fine.

Cheyenne: Mrs. May May, are you all right? Did you just say my *moms* are fine?

May May: Yes, love, I did. I am just fine, and so—

Cheyenne: I only have one mother, and she's across the street!

May May: Baby, you have two mothers. Please listen as I tell you the story of my life. Back when I was only sixteen, I was in love with this guy name Chad. He was so handsome and a basketball player. All the girls at school wanted him. They would go crazy. But I was not popular, and he pressured me for a date. One night I said yes. He took me out, and we had such a great day. He made me feel so good. I never had been on a date before, nor had I ever been kissed. He was so good to me that night, and I was so naive. I felt like I was on air that night and he was my wings. When we kissed, it was like a clear stream of water flowing with no interruptions. We ended up having sex under the stars, without any protection, and I became pregnant on my first time. With you, love. I am your mother.

Studae is at the liquor store and trying to order some cognac.

Studae: Gi-gi-gii … Gi-give m-me a b-b-boti of that y-y-y-yak, man!

Store clerk: Man, get out of here with your no-talking self. Trying to get more crap to make you not learn to speak at all. And slow down sometimes, man. Bad enough I can't make out what you say in time; now you want to rush it. Slow down, man!

Studae (still stuttering): I can say kiss my ass, fool. Now gimme that yak!

Sore clerk: That will be twenty-five good ones.

Studae: Thank you, fool.

Studae goes away to get his groove on.

CHAPTER 16

BOOTSIE JACKIE

BJ: Hello. Yeah, what's up, Maria, and what you doing?

Maria: I'm okay. I just wanted to holla and see what was up with you. But really I wanted to know why you keep pushing up on me, knowing I am not for it.

BJ: Ah, girl, you say that, and that is why you called to set it up. Okay, Maria. I am tired a little today, but we can hit it off tomorrow if so. Are you down or what?

Maria: I am not down, girl, and I won't be down. Look, I heard you were up to some shit, and I am not your reward. I want you to know that it ain't gon' happen ever. I am into men, girl. And I say it again: I am into men. You need to stop fooling yourself. As for trying to be hard, I see through you. It seems to be a front, BJ. Tell me what are you doing playing a man and not being what you are.

BJ: Look, Maria, why you calling and getting at me like this? All I have ever done was try to befriend you, but you have avoided me over and over. I think I have treated you fair day after day.

Maria: That is correct, and that is why I am not mad at you for me. But I am mad at you for this Shay shit. How can you turn my girl out, knowing you like men? I see the way you look at Paul. Hell, I seen the way you looked at Tricky Tee, and he needs a good woman to set his ass straight. But no, all you do is trip on females and hurt them. I heard that your last friend had to go the hospital because you were really rough with her, and now you hurt my girl Shay.

BJ: Wait, wait, wait! Hold on. I know Shay didn't confide in you about our secret. I told her ass to keep quiet in life.

Maria: Nah, you told her to keep quiet until you had me. But since I am letting you know it will never be you and I, I guess it was all right for Shay to talk to me. (Crying.) BJ, you hurt my girl. You hurt her bad. She can't sit still for nothing. I tell you, you better not have messed up her chance to have children. How could you be so mean to a girl like this? You are a girl yourself, and I know you wouldn't want anyone to hurt you. Am I correct, BJ?

BJ: I have been hurt.

Maria: What do you mean? You can talk to me. Look, you wanted me, so that tells you something of me. I am a friend to many and don't discuss their situations. Please tell me what is wrong.

BJ: You know, I think I need a friend to talk to before I hurt someone. Please meet me at the Applebee's on Airline in an hour.

Maria: Yes.

BJ: Where is Shay? I need to talk to her.

Maria: No, BJ. Not until I talk to you.

BJ: Cool. See ya in an hour.

Maria: Later.

Quotes of Life

If you forget what others have fought
for in life, you have lost in life.

CHAPTER 17

GIVING IT UP

Back at the house, Big Bo and Tulip meet up and remember the time.

Tulip: Big Bo, Big Bo, boy, is that you? What in the world? Come here, boy. Hug 'em up, big man; hug 'em up.

Big Bo: Man, what have you been drinking or taking a bath in, cousin? Man! Anyway, how about you let me buy you one, li'l cuzz.

Tulip: Never, Big Bo, I mean *never* will I turn down free gas. Ya heard me. (Laughs.)

They drive down the road.

Big Bo: Man, I hope you can handle the fuel that's being served.

Tulip: Man, oh yeah. But where are you going? Ain't anything around here but churches, man. You may want to turn around.

Big Bo: Man, we're going to have a big talk at the one place that's serves twenty-four hours a day.

Tulip: Man, bars close at two a.m., so stop tripping. But if you know such a place, let's get there. Come on.

Big Bo: Lord, build my strength to help my cousin.

Tulip: Boy, what are you praying about? Some alcoholics are something. Man, why are we here at this church? Come on, man; let's go in. Come on. Man, you brought me to a shot house behind a church. Man, I never knew. Let's go in. Come on.

Big Bo: Tulip, we're not going in until you're ready.

Tulip: Man, I am ready like Freddie.

Big Bo: If so, Tulip, take a knee with me. Let's pray for your freedom.

Tulip (staring): Big Bo, I know now what you're up to. I don't have a problem, man.

Big Bo: Man, you are the problem. You are in denial, cousin. Pray with me, Tulip.

Tulip (crying): Man, I don't have a problem.

Big Bo: Listen, Tulip. Do you remember when that family was killed in a car accident four years ago, across town?

Tulip: Yes, I do. Man, that was a sad day.

Big Bo (crying): I was the driver of the car that hit them.

Tulip: Man, no, you weren't. No, cousin, no. Not you!

Big Bo: Yes. And I had a problem called denial. The Lord saved me, and I want to help all in need of my help. It took a few lives to wake me up, and I am trying not to let anyone else travel my road. I spent four years in the state pen for my actions. I am trying to save lives, Tulip.

Tulip: Well, I understand, Big Bo. But I don't drive a car, man. I walk everywhere. And I am not drunk, can't you see?

Big Bo: You're in denial. No man is better than another, and I won't say that I am. But when alcohol becomes your life, you have to restructure your plans. You have a big problem, and everyone is aware of your problem.

Tulip (crying): I am okay, Big Bo. I am doing fine. I am happy, as you can see, man. My family loves me, Big Bo.

Big Bo: You may have a family, but do you have the Lord?

Tulip: In my heart, I think I have him. I think so, big cuzz.

Big Bo: If you believe, believe. If not, find him. With help, he's there, my friend.

Tulip: I want to change. I want to know him. But will he accept a man who has sinned for life? Will he take a broke-down drunk?

Big Bo: He has already forgiven your sins if you take him into your life. Now please, give me the bottle and take a knee with me, Tulip. (Crying.)

Tulip (crying): I am a good person, Big Bo. I am. I do no harm to anyone, cuzz. I do want the Lord. I do. Please help me.

Big Bo: Take my left hand and give me the bottle with your right. Now take a knee with me, cousin. Reach for what you want. Give me the alcohol.

Tulip: Oh Lord, help me. Lord, help me …

Big Bo: Pray, my brother. Pray with me. Please ask the Lord for what you want. Ask for help and it shall be received …

After a beautiful prayer, someone in the background yells out loudly.

Kim: Stop! Stop! Leave me alone, you damn fool. Move, stupid dummy.

Kim is drunk, as usual, but this time she is furious. Her friend has drunk all of the liquor that the two had purchased.

Kim: Isaac, why are you still here? I can get sober on my own. Act like Michael Jackson and beat it, fool. Just beat it. Dummy.

Isaac: Girl, stop playing and let's get back to unfinished business. We can go to the Club Bali for more juice. Come on, woman; come on.

Kim: Man, I ain't going nowhere. Ya make me sick. It's time for you to get gone. Get on, man. Get, get, get. Go on.

Isaac: Now, I ain't no drunken woman, so don't talk to me like that. (Singing:) I still have the Lord, yes, and he's got me.

Kim: The Lord? Fool, please. Don't use my Lord's name in vain. He is our Lord, and yes, he is, oh yes.

Isaac: I can back you there, girl. Hey, hey, hey, let's pray.

Kim: Boy, you're so stupid, but don't play with my Lord. Don't play.

Marcia, who is Isaac's wife, comes out of the church.

Marcia: No, no, no, you two. Don't play with my Lord. Why have you stood here, right outside of this church, drinking and playing as well as acting a pure fool? I don't know what you're looking for, but if you haven't found it by now, it's time for me to help.

Isaac: Girl, please go home.

Marcia: No, my husband. When I leave, we will both be heading home, together and with the Lord.

Big Bo: That's right.

Big Bo approaches them both.

Kim: Whatever. I think I will help myself to a drink, for the homeys.

Isaac: Holding out on me, huh? I see. Old, old, old fool.

Kim: Whatever, whatever! I got mine; do you?

Tulip: Kim, please put it down. It's time for all of us to stop.

Kim: Tulip, baby. How did you get down here? I . . . I . . . I . . .

Tulip: Shhhhh. Let it go, Kim. Please give it up and pray for forgiveness.

Marcia: Kim, please think of what you're doing. Please take my hand and kneel with me. Please.

Isaac: Marcia, I am sorry. I didn't mean to bother you. I am okay and headed home.

Marcia: Baby, please don't run. It's time to stop hurting me and our kids and, especially, my Lord.

Isaac: I haven't hurt anyone, only my lungs possibly. (Laughs.)

Tulip: Kim, they have a couple of problems to work out in the presence of my Lord, and we have to also work on our issues.

Kim: Did you say "my Lord"? Man, what's happening here? What's going on?

Tulip: Yes. My Lord. And he is yours also if you want. Please think of what you're doing.

Kim: What I am doing? He left me years ago when I was down, Tulip.

Big Bo: The Lord throws headaches at all of us to test our faith, and that was your test. Baby, I must say you've failed. Now that can be changed.

Isaac: I am still kind of lit, but I have a feeling someone sent them to us tonight, Kim.

Marcia: He's someone I love: it is my Lord. Do you know why we have lasted so long with your drinking problem? The Lord, that's why.

Isaac: You know, baby, you're right. It must have taken something to keep us together this long, because it sure wasn't me. Love, I am sorry. Please forgive me. Please.

Marcia: It's not me; it's the Lord you must ask forgiveness from. He is my Savior and can be yours also, if you want. Only if you want.

Kim: Lord, Lord, help me please, Lord.

Tulip: Take my hand. Take it. Don't turn him away again, Kim. Don't.

Isaac walks up and looks at Tulip, then grabs his hand while reaching back for his wife, Marcia.

Marcia: We have three; all we need is two for a team to battle the Devil.

Kim grabs Big Bo's hand.

Kim (crying): Big Bo, please walk with me to my love so we can pray together.

Everyone grabs each other's hands and kneels to the ground for prayer and a new beginning.

CHAPTER 18

CONFUSED TEARS

Cheyenne: Excuse me, you're my what? No way, miss; no way. My mother's name is Carroll. (Crying:) Why are you telling me this now? I have a mother. Please, Mrs. May May. Stop.

May May: I was young and my family had nothing to offer. Carroll offered to help in the situation. I agreed only if I could see you when I wanted. That's why I became known as your godmother. I wanted to be some part of your life, baby. I have loved you for sixteen years, and I am going to love you forever.

Cheyenne (crying:) So you're my mother? Oh God, help me. Please give me strength. You're my mother. My mom always said she wanted to have a woman-to-woman talk with me, and now I know why. She was going to let me know the truth. Mrs. May May, I love my mother and I don't want to leave her, and I love you also. I understand. Believe me, I do. I have been awarded an all-around terrific family. I have had you in my life this long, and I am going to have you more and more for life. I love you.

Cheyenne hugs May May.

Cheyenne: Oh my God. Mrs. May May is my mother, my real mother! Lord, I need to go home and talk to my mother. Oh my God!

May May: Baby, I used to sing a song daily to remind me that the Lord knows the truth. He is with me in my pursuit to win a part of my baby's heart as your real mother. I also sang above your crib when you were born.

Cheyenne: Well, Mother May May, can I hear a verse or two? I may remember the song.

Ms. Carroll enters the house, crying.

Ms. Carroll: Big Bo, why you had to do this to my child?

May May: Now come on, Carroll. You know it is time to reveal the truth. Cheyenne is sixteen and needs the truth. What if she gets hurt and needs blood or something, and I can't give her any because I am not her mother? She would eventually find out who gave the blood and be confused that I couldn't provide.

Carroll: Baby girl, I know you are confused and hurting in a way, but we both have loved you for so long and so hard. I must say that you have been the best daughter a parent could have ever had. Your grades have always been all As and you have never gotten into trouble. You have remained the best at everything you do, and never—yes,

Lord, I say never—did any drugs of any sort. You have been the angel child I could never have, and I have been so proud.

Cheyenne: Mom, it is okay. I love you so much for all that you have done for me. I will never leave your heart. I will never leave your home until it is time for me to go on in life. I want you to know that, although Mrs. May May is my biological mother, you are my mother. You have done that job since I was a little baby. I want to remain with you and love you for life itself. You are my joy. I will accept the truth with smiles. And I now have two great mothers in life. (Laughs.)

May May starts singing "I Know Who Holds Tomorrow" by Kelley Price.

CHAPTER 19

MARIA AND BOOTSIE JACKIE

Maria: Hi, girl. What's up?

BJ: Maria, I told you to not call me a girl. I am BJ, or you can call me my new name, Bootsie Jackie.

Maria: Listen, Jacqueline. I am going to call you a girl because that is what you are, even in this confused state of mind. Now stop and let's get down to business. I want to know what is wrong, and if I can, I want to help. For this I will refer to you as BJ, because it is cute like a girl, and you are a beautiful young lady.

BJ (laughing): Whatever, tramp. I know you mean good, but this is something I must carry out till the day they are all dead.

Maria: Who do you mean, "they"?

BJ: All who took me and did whatever they wanted to me and left me to grow up used and confused. I was hurt for nothing but mere crumbs. My mother took my youth, and now she lives this holier-than-thou life. I will make sure the truth is told on her. She will never get away with what she did to her only daughter. Now she sits up there and acts like all is good in her world. But Marcia David will pay.

Maria: What? You mean Mr. Isaac's wife Marcia? OMG! She is your mother. Oh my God. Girl, why didn't you say something? Did Mr. Isaac have his way with you?

BJ: No, not him at all. In fact, from what I see, he is a good man. But I don't know why he can't see the truth in her.

Maria: Now that I think about it, with your hair you do look like Mrs. Marcia. Oh God, how bad you must feel. And living right here in the same town!

BJ: I never left town. I cut my hair. I have plotted my revenge for nearly three years. I know who they are and where they all live. I will make them all pay. The ones who have families will suffer my loss. They live like nothing wrong has ever happened in their lives, but not anymore.

Maria: Girl, I am so sorry for that has been done to you. But you can't just kill people and expect to get away with it in life.

BJ: Who said kill anyone? Although they killed my youth, I want happiness, and they will pay. I mean *pay*, and I will start uptown tomorrow. It won't be a blackmail case. It will be a case of me having pictures. But I will get paid first and live my life happy.

Maria: So that is why you hurt the women you get with so bad.

BJ: I hurt them mainly to keep them away from me. But, like Shay, they keep coming back like I have some real penis in my pants. The more pain I inflict on them, the more they like it. I am really getting tired of trying to run them away. That is why I came after you, Maria: to give Shay a sign of me not wanting to hurt her anymore. But she took it as strong love. I don't get that, girl.

Maria: BJ, she fell in love with you and can't hide it.

BJ: Well, she better fall out, because I don't want to eat ass all my life. I want to be held and loved like every other woman, but my revenge has caused me not to focus on any man. I have not been penetrated in five-plus years. I live as a man, and that is that for now.

Maria: But tell me why not forgive and forget?

BJ: Forget! Girl, please. You don't have the smell of old-ass white men on you. You don't see or remember pain as I do. I live daily with what happened to me as a teenager. I hate myself for loving my mother enough to forgive her all while waiting for the pain to stop. I have tried and tried to move on, but the pain never stops. The men who laugh every day on TV will smile no more when I have my say.

Maria: Please tell me—what is your plan? If it doesn't include anyone getting hurt, I will help you. But if anyone is to be harmed physically, I am out. I also think you need to apologize to Shay and let her know who you really are. It will be for the best in life.

BJ: You are right. I will tell you this, but please never tell Shay. I do love her and want the best for her, but I can't be in a relationship with a woman forever. It is not part of my plan. I just had to create a false identity.

Maria: I want you to tell her everything, including the love you have for her. It will help in easing her pain.

BJ: You are right, and I will.

Maria: Now I need to get my girl together. I want you to call Shay and get her here with us. I will call Dee Dee. We have to get this done right, so they won't hurt another girl. This you can believe: never again.

BJ: Thank you, Maria. I really needed this talk and your words or else someone would have gotten killed. But I am still not right in life. I will need more words and maybe counseling to help me really. Yes, counseling. (Crying:) Thank you, girl. I am such a wreck in life. My mother doesn't care at all, but she will also remember and pay. I am going to church this Sunday to confess her sins. Okay, I will see you tomorrow. I have to call and speak to Shay. And Maria? I love you, girl …

Maria: Girl, I love you also. Now go talk to my girl and end this confusion now.

Quotes of Life

Don't forget what others fought for in life, and that is not stupidity.

CHAPTER 20

KATHY JEAN

Back at the house, the doorbell rings. It is Kathy Jean May, Lakeeba's mother. Grahams opens the door, and the healing continues.

Kathy (in a country accent): Good day, ma'am. I am looking for Ms. Mia-Duke Melbourne, whom everyone calls Grahams.

Grahams: This is she and you are Mrs. Kathy May.

Kathy: Yes, ma'am, I am. I was told my daughter could be found here.

Lakeeba, coming from the kitchen, hears her mother's voice and starts to cry. She runs to the door.

Kathy: Baby, oh my baby I am so sorry. Oh Lord! Oh Lord! Oh Lord, thank you for saving my child. Lakeeba, I am so sorry I took a no-good man's word over my baby.

Lakeeba: Mother, I told you and I told you. Why didn't you hear me? Why?

Kathy: I am sorry, baby. I only wanted a man in my life and at any expense. He was a liar. When you ran away, I knew nothing but to find my baby. I have been all over these states looking for my baby. It took the Lord to give me a sign.

Lakeeba: And what sign was that, Mother?

Kathy: That man went to church with me to pray for your safe return, only to touch a little choir girl as she went to the bathroom. It was all caught on camera, and he is now in jail.

Lakeeba: Oh God, he hurt others.

Kathy: No. He didn't get that far. But he was seen by the back office staff touching her body. They ran out and got the congregation, and we came to the little baby's rescue. I slapped him silly and told him how he had contributed to my blind eye and the loss of my child. Oh God, I hate him for that. But mostly I hate myself. He is in jail, doing five years' hard labor.

Lakeeba: Mother, you have said some hateful things to me over the years. Why couldn't you see the good in me, Momma? I was doing all you asked, and you treated me so wrong. (Cries.)

Kathy: I am sorry, baby. I was stupid. Please look in your good heart to forgive me. I will spend the rest of my life fighting for your love. I want my baby back. Please, Lakeeba. Please try to help me, and please forgive me. Please! (Cries.) Baby, please come home. I am so tired, running behind you. You have run to three cities, and I have been on your tail every step of the way. I want to take you home. I want my baby home. Everyone misses you, everyone. Please give me a chance to prove to you that I have changed. Please …

Lakeeba: Yes, ma'am. I want to come home. Mrs. Mia-Duke, could you please allow me to go with my mother? She needs me …

Grahams: Yes, dear. Things happen in this life that are not pleasant to all, but the Lord forgave and so shall you soon. The Lord has sent your mother. Please go find happiness with her. I will let everyone know that you have gone home. Get your bags, child.

Kathy: Ma'am, thank you so much for getting to that jail and getting my baby. I thank you for getting the counselor, Devin, to put out a missing person location line to Mississippi. I got the call and headed straight here. Thank you, ma'am. You are a real angel.

Lakeeba: I am ready, Mother. Mrs. Mia-Duke, thank you for your heart and opening up your home to me. My mother and I will find our happiness.

Grahams: Baby, you can't leave at this moment. There is someone who is coming to see the both of you. He should be here in a few. Please wait.

The doorbell rings. It is Chad, Kathy's ex-husband.

Kathy: What are you doing here, Chad? This is not the time. How could you show your face after all these years and all that we have been through? Leave now.

Grahams: Child, now stop and let the man make his peace.

Kathy: Mrs. Mia-Duke, he has been nothing to us all this time, and now he shows? OMG! How could you, Chad?

Lakeeba: Mom, what is going on? Who is this man you are arguing with, and about whom? Excuse me, mister, but please stop making my mother angry. Why are you here?

Chad: Listen, Lakeeba—

Lakeeba: How do you know my name? What's going on? I know you are not the police. Mrs. Mia-Duke came down and straightened things out. So why are you here? (Loudly:) Mom, please tell him I'm okay and he needs to leave.

Kathy: Chad, what you are doing?

Chad: I have been running around from state to state, trying to find my child after I found out she took off from you.

Lakeeba: Your child, sir? What and who are you speaking of?

Kathy: Lakeeba, it is okay, baby.

Chad: No, it is not. I want my baby girl to know me.

Lakeeba: Your baby girl? Sir, are you telling me that you are the man who hurt my mom and left me, your daughter, to suffer? I don't believe you showed your face. Why are you here, Mr. Chad? Why are you here? (Cries.)

Kathy: Baby, it is okay. And it will be okay as soon as we get out of here.

Chad: No, Kathy, it will not be. I have tried and tried to repent for what I did to you. I have suffered all my life without you. I have loved you from day one. I could never make it work with any other woman in my life because I loved only one woman, and that is you.

Kathy: Then why hit me and run me off with my child, *our* child, in tow? Why, Chad?

Chad (crying): I was stupid jealous and dead wrong. I am so sorry for what I have done, Kathy Jean. I swear to you, I am so sorry I hurt you and my baby girl.

Lakeeba: I am not your baby girl. I am a young lady who has made it this far without you. My mom and I don't need you, so please let us leave, mister, before it gets hot in here.

Grahams: Okay, now you all need to sit. (Loudly:) Sit, I say, and do it now, before the Lord releases me and I go off. *Sit.*

Everyone takes a seat.

Grahams: Now I went out of my way to give you your mother, Lakeeba. In the process, I found out who your father was and worked it so he could see his child. I did this not knowing any one of you. I did it out of the love I have for my Lord. He guided my hands into this situation, and I will see my Lord through on his words of guidance. I need for you all to listen to his holy word. Everyone, and I mean everyone, makes mistakes in life. Although we make decisions that hurt many in the process, we must ask for forgiveness. We must look deep within to forgive. Not forget, but to move on and make life easier for all involved. This man did not come over here to start a fight or bring pain to you, Kathy. He came to see his child and to formally apologize to her and you for what he done. He didn't ask to take his child from you and he didn't ask for Lakeeba to go with him. He simply said that he was sorry and wanted to ask for forgiveness and to see his baby girl. You, child, are running wild in your mind and need to slow down. Your father is here to help you make it in life. We all are not good in life every day, but we are okay. This man is asking for you to try and see him in a different light than what you have pictured him in. He is seeking you as his daughter and not his slave. Kathy, please try to reason with Chad. Please try to listen. This is not an attempt to get back with you. He is reaching for his baby, and you are blocking like you always have.

Kathy looks up.

Kathy: Chad, I am sorry for keeping your child away. I just wanted the best for her. I ended up becoming a punching bag for another guy who meant my child no good. And it turned out he was rotten to the core. I am so sick, knowing I lay with this man who had other thoughts in his mind. OMG! Lord, help me to be a better mother to my child. Oh, how I need you, Lord. Oh God, please help me to understand and live for you, Lord. Baby girl, come here.

Lakeeba: Mom, I am here.

Kathy: Baby, this man you see is your father and my first husband. And he is seeking a relationship with his child that I took from him. I ran away from the pain I felt in my heart. My life has been lived in fear and pain, but never again. I am strong and positive, and I am on top. I have my baby back, and I know I have the Lord. But the Lord wants you to have a heart filled with love for all and not just yourself. Chad, this is your baby I took from you. She is beautiful, strong, and confident like you. Please get to know her. Love her and be there for her. (Cries.)

Chad: Lakeeba, I know this is hard, and I know you have no love for me. But I am your father, and I want to get to know you for who you are. I want to help in making life positive for you. Baby girl, I need you so bad in my life. I hurt every day I can't see or hear from you. I have been a terrible man in life and life has shined its ugly light on me. I think I have been punished enough for what I became and what I did. I just want the chance to prove to all of my kids that I am here for you.

Lakeeba: What? I have sisters and brothers?

Chad: No, love. You have two brothers. They are sitting in the car, waiting to come inside and meet you if you will see them.

Lakeeba (crying): Mr. Chad, I will be honored to meet my brothers. I will be more honored to get to know you, my dad …

Lakeeba gets up and heads to her father. She extends her hand, and he grabs her and hugs her tight as they both cry.

Kathy places her head in her hands and cries.

Kathy: Thank you, Grahams, I mean Mrs. Mia-Duke. Oh my Lord, you don't know what you done for me, ma'am. Thank you.

Kathy goes over to Chad, hugs him, and tells him she is sorry for what she's done.

Chad goes to the door and motions for his sons to come into the house. Paul and J-Cob come inside and look into the eyes of Lakeeba whom they have seen many times at the club. They all smile and laugh.

Paul: Oh shit, you? You are the girl who I tried to holla at months ago. OMG! I am so glad God guided us away from each other.

J-Cob: Girl, I don't believe it. You are our sister. Man, what a small world. But what a wonderful day. Come here and give me a hug.

Lakeeba looks at J-Cob with timid eyes because she knows his secret. J-Cob tells her that it is okay. It is out. Laughing, they all say thank God and talk of the good, bad, and future times.

CHAPTER 21

JO-JOAN

While laughing and enjoying the moment, J-Cob's phone rings. It is Jo-Joan, and he is in no mood to be pushed away.

J-Cob: Hello?

Jo-Joan: Hi, J. It's me, and we need to talk now.

J-Cob: Jo-Joan, not now. It really is not a good time. I promise I will call you when I get out of here.

Jo-Joan: Girl, what now? Are you with another girl, trying to pass the time? I have been following you, and I am outside now. I seen Lakeeba hug on you from through the window. And to bring your dad and your brother with you to pass off like you are all man. Well, you are all man, *my* man, and I am tired of being pulled along.

J-Cob: Stop hurting me. Let me know what it is you want from me.

Jo-Joan: I am in love with you, and you know you love me. Why are you playing with me? *Why*!

J-Cob: Now Jo, I told you I would get back to you, and here you are going off on me for hugging my sister. Yes, my brother and father are here, meeting her for the first time.

Jo-Joan: What? You kissed your own sister? Damn, you are a trip and into incest. What kind of—

J-Cob: Shut up. I pecked her and that was to get you out the club. I did not know she was my sister, asshole.

Everyone looks on while the argument continues. Chad becomes irate with the whole situation and jacks the phone from J-Cob.

Chad: Listen, whoever you are. It's bad enough I have to accept this life my son lives. You're bothering us in a time of importance to everyone here. I need for you to call J-Cob back and that is that. *Do* you hear me?

Jo-Joan: Yes, sir. I am sorry. I am in love with J-Cob, and I didn't mean to cause any harm. I just need to know the truth about what he wants to do, because I have to move on in life.

Chad: Then move and don't wait for an answer from my boy.

The doorbell rings. Kathy opens the door and stands face-to-face with Jo-Joan.

Kathy: Can I help you?

Jo-Joan (standing with the phone in his hands): Yes. I am Jo-Joan. I need to see Mr. Chad and now.

Chad: I am here. What do you want now?

Jo-Joan: Sir, I have never disrespected you and your family. I steered away like I was asked to do by J-Cob. Now you take the phone and yell at me like I did something wrong. I have been who I am for over ten years, and I discovered who I was with a smile. J-Cob found me and not me him. I didn't barge my way into your family. I was escorted in by J-Cob. And you now blame me for your son being gay. I am not to blame for him being who he is, but I am to blame for keeping him who he is today.

J-Cob: Listen. Everyone, please, please listen. There is no need for any of us to get out of hand. I dealt these cards and now I must play the hand. I am a man with an identity issue. Until I find out who I am in life truly, I will keep to myself for the moment.

Jo-Joan: What do you mean, J-Cob? Are you saying you are going back to dating women only?

J-Cob: I am saying that I will become celibate for a certain period in time. That way I won't be hurting anyone, especially myself. I do love women, and I do love you Jo-Joan. I am not doing any good by living a confused life, and at this point in time, I am really confused. The things

I do with you, Jo, I can do with a woman. When I get with you, it is passion to the fullest but a real disconnect with me. I think I am just living out what happened to me in prison and not in life outside of the joint. I think that if I seek counseling, I can beat this issue with an identity problem. I wish you all the best in life, Jo. I want you to smile daily, but not with me. I need for you to let me go and find myself, as you should move on and find someone who will love you for you and not just for a moment. You and I have never been on a date in public, held hands, walked the beach, or done anything that a couple does. We have met behind closed doors. If I had been proud of who I was then, I would not have hidden in life. Please know that you are a good man, but we have to stop this lie between us now.

Chad: Thank God!

J-Cob: Nah, Pop. Thank Jo-Joan for being my friend and helping me come to this decision to change my life for the better.

Grahams: My Lord has been good to me, and I know he is being good to all of you who stand here today. Son, you must find your happiness. You all must kneel and pray for forgiveness at once. I tell you all to bow down to my Lord and see the light he has for you. If the light directs your path to remain as you are in life, then my God has spoken. But you must let go and let God do his work, for it is his will and not yours. Hallelujah, my God …

Grabbing Jo-Joan's hand, Chad leads everyone in gathering in a circle. They kneel and Grahams starts her prayer, asking for guidance and forgiveness of all their sins. Crying, everyone answers in unison, "Amen, amen, amen ..."

Quotes of Life

If you give up in life, you give up on others, and therefore you give up on God.

CHAPTER 22

HIDDEN AGENDAS

BJ: Hi, Shay, and thank you for coming over.

Shay has a sad and painful look in her eyes as she takes a seat.

BJ: I want to apologize for my actions in the past few months and how I treated you. You didn't deserve for me to be so rough on you and do what I did to you. I was hurting and wanted to hurt others. I am still hurting. I want you to know who I really am and what I have been through in life.

BJ explains her life and pain to Shay. Crying, Shay tells BJ that she did fall in love with her. Shay accepts BJ's apology and says she wants to help put the bastards who hurt her behind bars. Shay admits she only used BJ for the moment and that she wants to be loved by a man. She doesn't want be in this type of relationship anymore.

BJ: Our secret is only known by one other person, and that is Maria. She promised not to reveal anything. She only wanted me to be truthful in life and not hurt any more people. She also wanted me to work on my problems by seeking help.

Shay: That is Maria for you: stubborn as hell but also caring like no other. I love that girl now. Fill me in on what is going down starting tomorrow at this church.

BJ tells Shay the plan and helps her with the pain by taking care of her so gently, in a motherly way letting her how sorry she is. They laugh and tell jokes and work on the plan they will carry out after the church issue is resolved.

On Sunday, BJ wakes feeling relieved and free. She will see her mother for the first time in years and wants to look her best. BJ dresses in a stylish outfit she's purchased, looking nothing like her old self. She looks radiant and on top of the world, like she's stepped out of a magazine. She's as gorgeous as Halle Berry, and she looks in the mirror and knows it, coming to tears.

She gets herself together because it is time to reclaim her life. She will do that in thirty minutes. Maria, Shay, and Dee Dee call to make sure BJ is okay. She assures them that she is feeling happy today and can't wait to see her mother.

As BJ arrives at the church and prepares to step out of her SUV, a young man by the name of Travis Mitchell walks by, stops in his tracks, and offers her a hand out of her vehicle. Accepting Travis's hand, she feels like a queen. She greets him and says she will speak to him more after church. He proceeds into church, and she checks herself and sees it is time.

Catching her breath, BJ enters the church and goes to a middle pew. She sits and waits for the welcoming of visitors to the church. Then it will be show time. But she has to find her mother first, to make sure her plan will not be wasted. Looking around, she finds Shay, Dee Dee, and Maria sitting and smiling, all the while giving their approval of how beautiful she looks. BJ knows it and mouths thank you quietly.

The service is wonderful from the start. The lay reader does a wonderful job. The choirs sing the hymns like never before, as if God knows what time it is in this great church—BJ's mother's church.

The moment finally arrives. The girls stand and announce their affiliation and thank the church for having them. BJ sits, quietly wondering and having second thoughts. Then the lay reader, who is Travis Mitchell, looks straight at BJ and asks, "Do we have another?"

BJ steps out into the aisle and introduces herself. She asks the church if they mind if she makes a confession today. The church applauds and tells her to speak to the Lord, child. And BJ does.

BJ: First, obedience to God and my Savior, Jesus Christ. To the reverend, deacons, friends, family, and members of this great church, I say thank you.

Congregation: Amen!

BJ: I come today of my free will to express myself and to confess my sins.

BJ's mother is all smiles.

BJ: My name is Brittany Jacqueline James, and I am the daughter of Mrs. Marcia David.

Congregation: What? Ahh.

BJ: I want to confess my sins of engaging in sexual acts before I was married. I want to confess my sins of hurting others in life who did me no harm. I want to confess to my Lord how my virginity was stolen by sick men in this world. (Crying:) I want to confess the foul things that these no-good men had me do and did to me as a child.

The Reverend (standing and raising his hand): Speak on, child.

BJ: I want to confess how simple-minded I was in not reporting it. I want to tell the world how I was used for a simple dollar, all to satisfy a mere ego. (Shouting:) I want to express my hatred for my mother, who sold me to the lowest bidder in life!

Shay, Dee Dee, and Maria are now standing at her side and crying their hearts out.

BJ (also crying): I want my mother to come and stand by me and confess her sins to this church and to my Lord.

Marcia gets up and walks to her child, whom she has not seen in years. Marcia is crying her heart out.

BJ: I want my mother to stand here today and ask, not for my forgiveness, but for the forgiveness of the Lord in front of her peers, her friends, and her Lord. I want to hear you cry out to God and ask for forgiveness for what you did to me and made me become in life. Mother, I want the truth and only the truth. Please stop crying and tell this church how you gave me up to the devil.

BJ falls to her knees with her mother. She reaches for her mother.

BJ: Mom, I love you.

BJ kisses Marcia's hands. Then she rises and walks out of the church with her friends, all of them crying.

As they reach the door, Travis is on their heels.

Travis: Wait, wait, wait, BJ. I want to speak with you.

BJ turns around. She has tears in her eyes.

BJ: Why and what for? I am damaged goods.

Travis: Because you are God my Father's child, and we will get to know each other in Christ soon.

BJ and her girls march to their cars to continue to carry out their plan of repent and attack.

CHAPTER 23

THE PAYBACK

At BJ's home, the planning commences after all the girls have changed clothes and are ready for action.

Shay: BJ, are you okay? You really took it hard at the church.

BJ: I did, and that is because I felt the pain return to me. Then it was a feeling of relief as it was lifted off me and I was free.

Dee Dee: I feel so bad for your mother. I know you don't want to hear it, but I do for some reason.

BJ: Girl, no need to apologize. I feel bad about what I did, but it had to be done or I would have continued to hurt people and myself. She had to see the finished product of a happy young lady. Dang, girls, I feel so good. I know I am going to throw out all those manly clothes and wear my gear proudly. I have too many nice female clothes in here that are going to waste. But not anymore. I will prove this to my God: that I can make it in life and be happy. Thank you, my sisters. Shay, I really want to thank you for being my true spirit.

Dee Dee: Why thank her? She is like all of us and that is conniving at this moment.

Shay, Maria, and BJ laugh and ignore her question.

Dee Dee: What? What have I done? Forget it, you'll— Who's that walking up the steps? OMG! It's your mother, BJ, and she is accompanied by Deacon Travis.

The doorbell rings. BJ opens the door and looks at her mother with such disdain that it is a shame.

BJ: Why are you here, Mom? What in the world made you think I wanted you to come to my home? Hell, how did you know where I live?

Marcia: I always knew where you lived. I just couldn't gather enough courage to face my daughter that I hurt so badly in life.

Travis: Listen, BJ. It is right. Look, can we please come in and talk to you? I don't think this type of conversation should take place on your steps. I know you don't care for your mother at this point, but she is your mother.

BJ: You are right. I don't. You two can just leave!

BJ slams the door. Marcia lowers her head and looks at Travis.

Marcia: See? I knew this would not work. What am I to say to a child I used to gain in life? What, Deacon? Please tell me. I want my daughter back in my life, and now I know it will never be. I—

The door opens.

BJ: Mom, why did you let them hurt me? I was a fifteen-year-old. I didn't know anything in life. I was an A student and did whatever you asked of me. It was you and I without my father. I loved you so much that it hurt me to think of losing you in any way. I wanted you to stop them from hurting me. But you never came to me. You never opened that door and pulled a nasty old man off of me. You treated me like a piece of property that you had thrown out. Mom, what did I do to make you treat me that way? I never hurt you. I respected you. I kept the house clean and never talked to boys. I was a good girl, Mom, but you took that away from me. You took my childhood before I was ready. (Cries.)

Marcia: Baby, I am sorry for what I done to my baby. I am so sorry … I panicked and I was scared in life. We were suffering, basically, in a bad situation. I was a call girl, BJ. I sold myself for a dollar. I wanted to be on top, and I got there by lying on my back. I never told you where I was going or what I was doing. I just did it and thought nothing of it. I was taking care of my child. Whatever a man or woman requested of me sexually, I did. I was nothing in life but a simple whore. I gave you the best and I tried to reason with myself that I was doing what I did for you. Baby, I am so sorry for what I did. I didn't think like a mother. I thought like a common whore in the streets. I was after the money and wanted to live on top of the world. I wanted my baby girl and me to have it all. I gave my soul to the Devil in giving my child up to fulfill the fantasy of some men. I thought you would like it in some way and appreciate what we were getting financially to live the lavish lifestyle. I didn't think like a mother.

BJ listens and sobs while her mother speaks. Travis looks on with wide eyes, shocked by hearing Marcia's story.

BJ: Mom, you used me for your private gain, not mine.

Marcia: I did, baby girl, and I am so sorry for what I have done to you. Look at you. OMG, you are so beautiful and seem so at peace.

BJ: At peace, Mom? I don't think so. I hurt people, and I damn sure used them like you used me. I made friends of mine not want to be friends with me. I didn't give a damn because I was after mine like you were after yours. As they say, like mother, like daughter. I damn sure was you, Mom. Or should I call you by your first name, because I don't have a mother? Ms. Marcia.

Marcia: OMG! My Lord, please take me away from this earth. I can't do it myself. I can't hurt myself. But you, Lord, you can make the call to end this miserable life. I have nothing to live for, God. I want it to stop, God. Please stop the pain. I don't want to live anymore, Lord. Please God, take me out of my misery. It has to stop one day. God, haven't you punished me enough in life? I have no life, no love, no happiness at all, and no daughter. (Falls to her knees.)

Travis: No. My God will not take your life. My God will only help in life, and he wants to help you. He *will* help you, and he will restore your relationship with BJ. Just be patient. It will be soon, Marcia. Soon it will be. I pray for you and stand with you. I believe in you. I need for you to raise your head and look to the Lord for help.

BJ (screaming): Stop it, stop it, *stop it!* I don't want to hear it anymore. I want you to take this woman and leave, Travis. I don't need her in life. I need for you two to leave!

Travis: No, BJ. You must let your mother ask you for forgiveness. It is the only way in life that will begin the healing for the both of you.

BJ: The healing? I will never heal. How can I forget what was done to me? How can you live a luxurious life that is filled with lies, Mother? I can't understand how you could be in any relationship and not talk of your child. I am your daughter that you raised until I was fifteen. Then you put me out there to make money for you like a tramp. And I was so stupid. I did it out of love for you. You said to me over and over that is was to help us make it in life. The money was to help me in college. But no, not college. It was not to be. I had to struggle daily in life just to make it after lying on my back for a hundred thousand-plus dollars. I helped you all right, Mom. I helped you destroy me. But it ain't over. If God takes you away from this earth today, at least I have gotten the last word. Now get the hell off my porch, woman!

Maria runs up and grabs hold of BJ, who is ready to attack her mother.

Maria: No, BJ. Please stop before you lose it. Please stop and think of what is happening. You know the deal, and that is why you are fighting it. You know that God wants you to forgive your mother. Her standing here today is a true testament to life. I think you need to calm down and think about everything that has happen in life to this date.

BJ: Maria, she hurt me so bad. I grew up confused and lonely, wanting my mother to hold me, to love me, and to care for me. Mom, I loved you so much, and I still do love you. I just can't let it go. I want to, deeply. I truly do, but I can't. I feel I want blood to spill and not yours. As for those nasty men who took advantage of a little girl, I want them dead. They forced themselves in me daily for fake pleasure. I want them to pay, because I know they have hurt many more young women.

Marcia: Baby, I was hungry for status, and I used everyone I came in contact with. I used your father, and then he found out I was selling my body and left me pregnant and in the cold. I stopped to have you, but when I was able, I was back out there getting mine. I didn't give a damn. I was just no good to anyone. I admit to you that I used you, baby. I just wanted to smile in life and not suffer or struggle. I had no skills. I only had a body and great looks.

But what is a whore to do with a child? I had to pay for babysitters daily to watch you. Those ladies were not your aunts, but prostitutes I paid to watch you on their days off. They charged me dearly because you were a needy child.

BJ, with tears in her eyes, smiles at her mother.

BJ: Mom, no matter how you put it in words, you used me. I put up with it for a year until I ran off. Now you want me to forgive you as if nothing happened and live a happy mother/daughter life. Well, Mother, tell me how I can just move on in life without thinking back and crying daily over my lost childhood?

Marcia: Baby, I don't have the answers. But I do have love to give and God to help us build. I know we can't be like the Bradys in life. But I want to be able to hold my grandchild one day.

The girls laugh, knowing the deal with BJ.

Marcia: Baby, please try to find empathy for me and forgiveness in some way. I won't ask for anything. I don't need anything, and I am not talking financially. I am talking about not needing you to be with me every day. I just need for you to know me again as your mother and not the lady who hurt you. Baby, if I have to turn myself in to the authorities for what I did, I will, because I have to pay my debt to everyone. I was wrong. You let it be known today in church, and I welcomed you with open arms to speak clearly and release the pain.

Travis: That is right, BJ. Your mother said that you would come with some terrible news to deliver to the church, and you did. The church is still in limbo from the service today. We had to end service early because people cried so much, and we know why. You left your mark in church today. Your mother needs you to help her redeem herself in the eyes of the Lord.

BJ: I need my mother to help me find those bastards who placed dollars in a starving woman's face and asked to rape her daughter over and over for a year.

Marcia (crying): I will, BJ. I will help you take this nasty empire down, because they have not stopped.

BJ: How do you know this?

Marcia: Because I was a madam to many girls who have come and told me of the things they do to underage girls. My girls said that when they arrived for a session, a young girl would be sitting there. They were ready to walk out the room and were offered up to fifty thousand to stay, and they did. Some regretted it, and some loved it because the dollar speaks volumes in life. I eventually gave up the madam gig and started focusing on my life and repenting for what I have done. Being in my forties signaled a time for me to stop and think about all the people I hurt: the wives, the kids, and the parents of the young girls who worked for a dollar. Once I left, I was called and threatened not to open my mouth or die a slow death. They even threatened your life.

BJ: What? How did they know where I lived?

Marcia: They have ways, BJ, and that is how I knew where you lived. They gave me the address and told me to check it out for myself. I drove by one day and seen you and started to cry. I wanted to get out and run to you. But I knew you would have had a fit and spat on me. I vowed to protect you by keeping my mouth shut and letting you live your life. But let me say this: I am not ashamed of you for living as a lesbian.

Dee Dee: What?

Shay: Shut up, girl. Like you didn't know.

BJ: So they want me dead if you help others?

Marcia: Yes, baby, and they were serious.

BJ: We have to take this nasty empire down, Mom, and now. I need you to help me, and I mean help me now. I can't go on in life letting another young girl suffer at the hands of some perverts.

Marcia: I will help all I can. I am not scared. But I want you to be very quiet on this and what we will be doing. Are these young ladies a part of your plan, BJ?

BJ: Yes, they are, and they are cool. But you need to know one thing, Mom. I can't forget, but I will try. For the sake of my God, I will try.

Travis: I am a man of God, but this calls for me to help stop this travesty. I will devote my time to helping to end this ring of terror against the young.

BJ: Mom …

Marcia: Yes, BJ …

BJ runs to her mother, grabs her tightly, and never wants to let go. Everyone is crying and in a state of disbelief as they see something they didn't think would happen.

Quotes of Life

Live out your script, for life is written.

CHAPTER 24

EXPLOSION

Paul has heard that Raul tried to pull a fast one on his girl Maria. He didn't take the news very well. He feels it was his fault. The next week, Paul and Raul run into each other but not by accident.

Paul: Raul, man, what has got you living the way you do? I thought at first about paying you with a bullet, but my Lord enlightened my intentions. He told me to use the holy words, which would penetrate much deeper and help much more. Man, I think—

Raul: It's time you let me speak. Paul, man, I was on that stuff and wasn't thinking straight. Man, I really liked Maria, and I am sorry for trying to violate her. I am so tired of living this crazy life. (Crying:) I want some help. I need some help. Please forgive me, please. I have been so wrong, and I want to change. Please help me.

Paul: Give me your hand, Raul. Now, my cousin, let's pray. I forgive you.

Meanwhile, at a party, everything is going well and no one's in a bad mood until Nicole arrives and Shay catches her eye.

Shay: Dee Dee, what in the world is she doing here? I thought this party was for the normal crowd.

Dee Dee: Maria, did you invite her? Girl, I know you're not starting up mess again.

Maria: Look, fools, I don't know nor have I set anything up. I am also not going to pick between friends and family. I am who I am and not who you want me to be, all right? Man, I am out of here. Later.

Maria walks away with an attitude.

Nicole: Shay, Dee Dee, how are you tonight?

Dee Dee: Fine, Nicole, but what are you up to? It hasn't been a week, and now you're back.

Shay: Okay, Nicole, what is it?

Nicole: Look, Shay, I want to apologize for interfering in your relationship with your man, Tim. But I was and I still am in love with him. I know I need to let him go. I also know he loves you. Shay, I am sorry for attacking you. It was childish, and I was jealous seeing you hugged up with him. I also shouldn't have lied to Maria about being with him, because he loves you and would never let me come between you two. I am so sorry. I wish you would please forgive me for my actions. Please forgive me, Shay.

Shay: I forgave you the moment you started to go off at the mouth. I knew it was jealousy coming out, and that's why I didn't fight back so much. I played it off. Please forgive me for anything I have done to you in the past. By the way, I am not with Tim and have not been for a while. He was history to me, as he was coming between my friends. I don't need a man breaking up the girls. I love you,

Nicole: And I love you too, Shay.

Tim comes walking up.

Tim: Nicole, what's up? What do you mean, it's over? Please stop playing.

Shay: It's all right, Tim. We were just talking, and she and I are okay about the situation.

We have forgiven each other, and we forgive you for bothering our life. Everything is all right.

Tim: Thank you, Shay, but please butt out. Nicole, is this true that you want nothing to do with me? I thought we had something.

Nicole: Tim, what we had were lies full of lust. I am not for this anymore. I have moved on, so please let it go.

Tim: Okay, Nicole. I see that it is over. Being the man I am, I will accept that. But please know—and I say this to all of you—I never meant to hurt any of you. I hope we can all be cordial and friends in the end.

Everyone: That is cool …

Tim: Okay then, I guess I will be out. I will talk to you later.

Nicole: Talk to you later, and Tim, can I have a hug?

As they hug, Nicole's new beau is off in the distance, looking on but confident in their love for one another. He simply waits for everyone to leave and drives up to Nicole. He rolls down his window.

New beau: Hi, love. How are you?

Nicole: I am fine and ready to go. I thought they would never leave. Baby, guess what? I let Tim and the girls know the deal. I didn't want to lead them on anymore, as if I was still with Tim. I want to be with you. Soon all will know that we are one and mean business.

New beau: I really love you Nicole and I can't wait to hold you. Please know how much you mean to me. I just want the best for us, and that is why I have not come out and told many people. Also, I wanted you to have the time to tell Tim to back off. And you have. I watched from across the street at how he was questioning you. I started to drive up, but I seen you had a handle on things. The hug was cute but understandable. Baby, it is you and I and no one else. They all will see soon. I promise you that they will be shocked but enjoy our passion for one another.

Nicole: That is true. Now park that car and get in mine and ride with me to our spot. I have a plan of attack for you … (Smiles.)

New beau: No problem, love. Wait one.

He parks and jumps into Nicole's ride. They head off into the night to make passionate love until it is time for Nicole to go home, relaxed and in love.

Meanwhile Maria has left the party, only to be followed by Pep, who was told to keep an eye on her. She is headed to Paul's house, but she is met by Mrs. Carroll, who was called by Grahams, who was called by Pep once Maria exited the party. Paul lives a few houses down from Mrs. Carroll.

Carroll: Baby, it's late. Where are you heading this time of night?

Maria: Hello, Mrs. Carroll. I am headed to Paul's house. Do you know if he's home?

Carroll: Child, he left about half an hour ago with friends, headed to a party. But please come in the gate, baby. I want to talk to you.

Maria: Yes, ma'am.

Carroll: Baby, I hear you have been on a rampage lately, creating a lot of confusion. I have wanted to talk for a long time now, and I am glad to see you tonight. (Laughs.)

Maria: Mrs. Carroll, I don't think so, ma'am, I have not been a problem or any trouble. So excuse me, ma'am, but what are you talking about?

Carroll: Your behavior, child; your behavior. Baby, you act as if the world is against you, and it is not.

Maria: I really think this world is for the birds. No one understands us young folks at all. We are always told we are wrong, and that is not the case. No one listens at all, Mrs. Carroll. People are always trying to live your life for you.

Carroll: Baby, I think you're wrong there. No one is trying to live your life for you. Your life is already written, child. Most people today are trying to save the young ones' minds from corruption and drugs. That's why you're still here, love. Someone cared.

Maria: Yes, ma'am. I have been a handful bad lately. Have you heard anything good of me at all? (Crying:) I am not all bad, Mrs. Carroll. I do have some good qualities.

Carroll: Baby, what's wrong? Are you really that upset with yourself, or just plain negative toward the world?

Maria: No, it's not that, ma'am. I am just so tired of trying to please everyone. My friends, my family, and my man. I even lost my job.

Carroll: But I know one thing you have not lost, and he's the Lord, baby.

Maria: Mrs. Carroll, who will I be able to call when in need? Every time I try to go and talk to someone, they think I am just whining. I am not. I may play around, but who can I call that will listen and not judge? Who will be there for me? Mrs. Carroll, who can I call?

Carroll: Baby, you can call on the Lord. Yes, my child. You can call him.

Mrs. Carroll starts to sing and deliver a positive message. Once the song is complete, Maria runs to Mrs. Carroll. They both drop to their knees and began to pray.

Back at the house, the family awaits the arrival of Maria and Mrs. Carroll. All members are there. Raul and Paul have also come by to wait for the deliverance of Maria to adulthood and the Lord. The door opens, and everyone greets the two who are covered with joyful tears. After hugs and praises, Raul approaches Maria.

Raul: Maria, I am sorry for my stupidity. I was wrong to take advantage of your friendship. I just was into that garbage. But I am free now, completely free. Please forgive me.

Maria: The Lord holds no grudges, nor do I. I forgive you, Raul. Thanks for coming over to do what you have done: apologize in front of my family. Thank you.

Paul: Maria, my love, I too am so sorry for abandoning your trust and not standing by your side in time of need. Please forgive m—

Maria: Baby, forgive *me* for not respecting our friendship and our love. Please forgive me.

They hug and smile.

CHAPTER 25

THE TAKEDOWN

Mr. Tom Wills, Mr. Jake Seamier, Mr. Samuel Miller, Mr. Robert Thompson, Mr. Gregory August (which rings a bell with BJ because he always asked for her every two days), Derrick Jones, and Bobby Matthews are all to be taken down.

Travis has called in one of his buddies and a member of the church, Detective David Dickens. David is a real pro and keeps rubbing his hands in anticipation of the takedown. He knows this will surely lead to a promotion, as this is his biggest case ever, but it has to go down correctly. He takes the lead in the plan of attack, in which he will use the girls as bait.

David: Okay, Dee Dee. Marcia will set it all up. She will place a call telling the NBs—

BJ: Yes, nasty boys.

David: The NBs will fall for Marcia's new company, which specializes in little girls. Dee Dee and Shay will capture all on tape and camera. But I want this to be the truth. I want you girls to be on point and not scared. Marcia, I want you to get all of them together for a trip-type of orgy throwdown. Tell them that you have four girls who will be down for whatever and whoever wants to play. Also tell them that this will be the night of all nights. The cost for each participant will be a million dollars, and this party will last three days. Tell the NBs that the only things that will be required are constant showers and the serious use of protection. There will be no holds barred on this one. Maria, Dee Dee, and Shay, can you get away for this sting, or do we need to talk to your parents beforehand? We don't want any problems, and we can get other girls if so.

Maria, Dee Dee, and Shay (in unison): No, sir. We are all willing to help our friend.

David: Fine. Here is the deal. I will turn my head in the end. If you help in taking down the NBs, the money will be split up to help you all in life.

The girls all agree as they mentally count the money. This will not be a lie; it will be a donation to the church and to the girls, who are doing a great deed.

Marcia is on the phone.

Marcia: Hello, Derrick, and how are you?

Derrick: I am fine, Marcia. What can I do for you?

Marcia: Well, Derrick, I am back and on fire. I have some ripped and ready youngies who are willing to take this shit to another level. They just need the right players to pull it off. I have four off-the-chain cuties who are all cuties and ready to make some money. Not any money, I may add, because this party is going to last three days, and it will be nonstop sex any and every way you all want it. One, two, and three at a time. They just want to get paid, and I want the money myself. I am starting on a bang, and I need the funds to create this empire. I am through with trying to be good. I want you to know that I am back, baby.

Derrick: I know you are not back in the sex game yourself, are you?

Marcia: Hell nah; those days are over. I want to get paid. Since you guys like to spend your hard-earned cash on young ass, I will ensure that you have a new piece every week. It is my time to shine, and I got the right stash of girls. You can try up to fifty, and I still will have about a hundred more for you to get at. Try me and see, Derrick. Now I want you to get your boys together and rent out a nice, big house that has about eight rooms. They all will be used. I will supply the maids and the butlers to clean after every session. One more thing: the maids are also down if you want to pay extra. They will be older, but hey, old whores need cash also. (Laughs.) So hit me back if you are interested. Bye!

Derrick, in amazement, gets on e-mail and starts to set it up. He knows that Marcia was one of the best and always brought the best to a party. His boys know and remember the times they had.

Derrick's e-mail, using code words:

> *Chichi, the time has come for our weekend getaway. This is to be a bang of a good time. All that will be needed is a change of clothes and stationery items. Marble and his gang will be the host. Bring all the rubber cups you can. In case you are wondering who will be there, about one million little sea fish are ready to be taken. Get back at me if you can come on this trip. Plane leaves Friday the 29th at 4 p.m.*
>
> *Later, D*

Immediately the responses come from all the players, because they know the deal. Being millionaires, the one million dollar tab for each person is not an issue.

Marcia: Okay, people, it is on. They will get the same house they always get, so we have time to set up the cameras and recording equipment to catch their asses in the act, as well as get confessions.

BJ: Mom, truly, thank you for helping me to put an end to this nasty game.

Marcia: It is my duty and my honor to help in restoring your dignity. And BJ …

BJ: Yes, Mom?

Marcia: Baby girl, I love you.

BJ: I love you too, Mom.

David: Maria, Shay, and Dee Dee, here is the plan. I want you to listen closely, because this will be a very serious situation. You will be in the house alone with the perverts. We will, however, have boys in the attic, waiting to come down and take out whoever tries anything. We will meet once a week for the next three weeks to prep for this. I will not confide in anyone. Everybody has a price, and I don't want to tip off anybody. When the time and date comes, I will tell my peeps to hold me down on a favor, stake out, and make our move.

Everybody agrees and heads home. Marcia and BJ remain to talk and try to rebuild their torn life.

Quotes of Life

The Devil failed you, your family loved you, and God saved you.

CHAPTER 26

PEP, MIKE, AND STUDAE

Jerry: What have I been waiting for all this time? For her to tell him that she loves Paul, Come on, people. That can't be true. Man, man, man, what in the world?

Giselle: Now, Jerry, calm down. It just wasn't to be, so please calm down.

Jerry: How can I when my baby is hugging on that guy? He doesn't look half as good as me. What in the world are you thinking, Maria?

Giselle: Jerry, it's *okay*!

Grahams: Baby, please come over here and let me say a few things to you.

Jerry: Yes, ma'am.

Grahams: Jerry, the Lord has plans. This was not written. Therefore, when it's not to be, it's not to be. Please calm down, baby, and accept the fact that she is in love with Paul.

Maria: Jerry, Jerry, please look at me.

Jerry: Yes, my— I mean, Maria.

Maria: I do love you and that will never change, but I am *in* love, totally, with Paul. We will be joining as one someday. Please understand my heart and not your wants.

Jerry: Well, Paul, you better do all you can to take care of my— I mean, that beautiful woman. Because if not, I— I mean, *someone* will be waiting.

Paul: Thanks, man. And I understand. I do.

Paul reaches out for Jerry's hand.

Jerry: I still am going to watch you, Paul.

Pep and Mike and Jo-Joan come into the house.

Pep: Okay, now I see what the looks were about. Jo-Joan and I were thought to have been hugging and me gay or something. Well, people, I am not gay.

Jo-Joan: No way in the world. But perception can kill a hard man. I was broke down when I heard the truth from Studae—what I could make of what he was saying.

Pep: Mike and I were talking in a room of nosey people, so some of our words were taken out of context. I told him about when I had to defend Jo-Joan that afternoon. No, people, I had no weapon on me. I faked like I had one, but I didn't reveal anything. I don't own a gun. I was only looking out for family, and no matter what, Jo-Joan is family.

Studae: What do you mean, fool? I shouldn't have told you nothing. I should've let everyone think your yellow behind was bent. Shut up and give hugs, man. Shhhhhhhut up!

Everybody: Shut up, Studae!

Maria: Grahams, where is Lakeeba? She doesn't want to come out of her room?

Grahams: No, baby. Her mother came, and so many tears were shed that there was a lake. She is on her way home with her mother to rebuild. Her mother took her home with nothing but remorse and love. And get this: her father and brothers were also here, and they all left happy. By the way, people, Lakeeba's father is Chad, and her brothers are Paul and J-Cob. (Laughs.) My Lord, you are so good … Now Giselle and Big Bo have something to say, and I want it heard loud and clear. Maria, come here, child. May May, it is now time.

Big Bo: Maria, back in high school I played ball and was on top of the world. Then I met this beautiful young cheerleader, and she was my heart. I, on the other hand, had other plans.

Maria: Oh my Lord. Big Bo, are you saying you are not Big Bo, my cousin, but Big Bo, my father?

Big Bo: Yes love. I am your father.

Maria becomes dizzy and takes a seat.

Maria: OMG! How in the world do people do things like this and expect it all to be good in the end? My God! Here I am hating my father, but yet loving him because he has been in my family all this time. Mom! Why? Please tell me why.

Giselle: Baby, embarrassment …

Maria: What?

Giselle: Big Bo grew up in the family. We thought he was kinfolk for years. But it turned out that, instead of him being my first cousin, he is like my fifth, if that. But mainly he is a family friend who calls himself cousin to us. For over fifty-plus years, we have thought we were really related, but we are not. When Big Bo got out of prison—

Maria: Prison? I thought you were traveling.

Big Bo: No, people. I did time for hit and run. I killed a family with my stupid drinking. I wronged a family, and I am still paying for it every day. I pray and pray for forgiveness. (Cries.) That is why I am here: to right all the wrongs in my life and help others before they end up suffering like I have in life. I come here to help you, Maria.

Maria (crying): Big Bo, why did you not let it be known? I needed you as my father and not a distant cousin. OMG! I don't know if I should hate or love you, but I know I am so upset with you. Mom, what am I to do? How can I open my heart to love my cousin as my father?

Giselle: The Lord will help us, and mainly you, Maria. He knows best. That is why it was time to get everything out and let Big Bo claim his rights as your dad.

Maria: My dad? Come on, mom ... How long have you all been plotting this headache you have caused me today? I thought it was all love a minute ago, and now I am confused, hurt—and somewhat happy. So you thought you were first cousins and still did the nasty and created me, and then hid the truth for years. What in the world, Mom?

Giselle: Baby, we didn't want you to go through life being teased. Now you won't. Although it took so long to tell you, Big Bo has always provided and been there for you more than you know. He shopped with you, talked to you of life, was there at many events of your life. He wanted to let you know and thought of telling you before he got locked up for the accident.

At that point, he didn't want to bring you pain and more embarrassment over your father being in jail. But now it can be different. We are not kinfolks at all. We are just family by association, and he is your father. Please try to see the good in him for what he didn't do and what he is doing now, Maria.

Maria (crying): Big Bo, if you are my father, then tell me my birthday, my favorite color, what I am afraid of, and who I love the most in life.

Big Bo (crying): Baby girl, your birthday is April 15, your favorite color is blue, you are afraid of spiders and rats, and you love your mother more than anything in life.

Maria runs to Big Bo. She hugs him as they all cry.

CHAPTER 27

TRAVIS

Maria, being the negative one in a way, once again has her life in order. Now the day is fast approaching when she will need to keep her promise and help take down the men who violated her friend BJ. The smile that arises on Maria's face is happiness like being rescued from deep water.

Shay: Girl, what is up with you today after that beautiful gathering yesterday at your house?

Maria: It seems like everyone is being blessed in one way or the other. I can do nothing but smile.

Shay: But Maria, can I tell you something?

Maria: Yes.

Shay: Well, I miss BJ so much. I know it is over, but I truly fell in love with her. I know she was not trying to hurt me. I seen the hurt in her eyes the many times we got together. Now I know what it was, and I feel more comfortable in life knowing it wasn't me that was causing her to pull away.

Maria: Look, Shay, I want you to get it out of your mind and concentrate on life with a man. Because it won't be with BJ anymore. She made sure of that. And did you see the way Travis interacted with her on the many occasions we have been meeting? He seems to like her a lot.

Shay: I know, and that is why I find myself getting jealous a little.

Maria: Well, Ms. Confused, come back to earth. She wants to be held and not caressed all the time. (Smiles.) I know you mean good, Shay, but life moves on and so should you. Now, if it turns out that you want to remain in the gay world, find another person who is willing to share in your life. But leave BJ to grow and find herself. If she feels that her love for you can't be forgotten, maybe there will be a chance. But truly, let it go, Shay.

Shay: I will try, but she looks so damn good now. You see how she just switched it and walks with a shake? Go 'head now, girl. Get it, get it! (Laughs.) I know, right?

Travis: Hello, BJ, and how are you doing today?

BJ: I am fine, Travis, and you?

Travis: Well, I have been okay. Just wondering how you have been holding up with all this rehearsal stuff in taking down the bad guys.

BJ: I have been good. I just feel so blessed in trying to rebuild with my mother. She and I have been inseparable these days. She seems so sorry for what has happened in my life. I am really starting to feel that this can work out for all of us. I mean, mistakes happen, and people make up for them daily. My mother seems to really want this in life. It's like she has no time left. She calls daily, wanting me to know what she is doing. I don't need a report daily, but she wants me to believe in her and learn to trust her again in life. I feel so blessed to have her again. Oh, excuse me. I am ranting on and on, and you called me. So back to you. What have I done to receive this call from you at 9:20 p.m.?

Travis: I wanted to talk with you and be open in life with you. I feel a connection growing between us. It started that day when I seen you looking so beautiful stepping out of that SUV. I just remember looking into your eyes and wondering who this beautiful young lady could be. I mean, I am twenty-one and a junior deacon, but not really a deacon. I am more like a lay reader who conducts church. What I mean to say is that you are eighteen …

BJ: What are you getting at, Travis? This is not that type of party. I thought you were different. Just because I was using back—

Travis: Hold up, BJ. I meant no such thing. Please let me finish. I was saying that you are eighteen and soon to be nineteen in a few weeks, right?

BJ: Yes, and how did you know?

Travis: I asked your mother.

BJ: Okay. I see. You checking up on me.

Travis: Nah. I am trying to get to know the woman I feel a connection with. I just turned twenty-one, and so I am a little over two years older than you. I wanted to see if you would allow me to date you or, as they say, court you. I really like you, BJ. I know you had a very difficult young life, and I know you gave your all trying to figure out who you were in life. I understand, and I can identify on many levels you may not believe.

The line goes quiet.

BJ: Travis, are you there?

Travis: Yes, I am. I am just thinking of my life. Would you like to get a late cup of coffee? I really need to talk to you and let you know of me face-to-face. Please …

BJ: Travis, it is getting close to ten o'clock. Where would you like to go at this time? I am not dressed. If I were to come out, it would take me an hour to get dressed.

Travis (somberly): Okay. Maybe tomorrow.

BJ: Look. You seem like a very nice man. What could be so important that you can't tell me on the phone?

Travis: My life, BJ. I want to open up to you about my life.

BJ: Okay. I feel that there is something very serious here. I want you to come to my home. We can talk, but not too long. We all have a busy day tomorrow rehearsing for the sting operation. How long will it take you to get here?

Travis: About forty-five seconds.

BJ: What? Stop playing, Travis.

Travis: I am not playing. I drove to your home, hoping you would agree to meet me. I am not stalking you. I really wanted to see you. I have been pacing all day, trying to come up with a line to get you out the house. But please, only for a little. I have to talk to somebody, and that somebody is you.

BJ: You really sound hurt. What is going on with you?

Travis: I have been through a storm like you, but I have never opened up about it. I have walked around and acted like my life was okay. I have been much protected and have done what I could to make it in life. I live on my own and have done so for over three years now. I left home early to start out on my journey to prosper in life. I have been abused like you, BJ. My father was an asshole and treated me like a whipping boy. He beat me at random and didn't let me do anything.

I never played any sports. All he wanted me to do was work the farm back in North Carolina. My hands would bleed every day from working in the fields, and then my behind would bleed from being abused by a crazy man. My father did ten years in the pen for attempted murder, got out, and was okay at first. Then my mother died, and he was left to take care of me. He started drinking more and not doing the job in the fields he used to do. When I became sicteen, he forced me to stop going to school and put me to work in the fields, saying a man earns his keep. I worked day and night. If he didn't feel I'd done my share, he pulled the whip, an old-fashioned whip, and beat me red like a slave. I remember crying and asking God, "Why am I being abused like this?" only not to be answered in life. Instead I was beaten more for praying to a God my father didn't believe in at all. He blamed God for taking his wife and making him suffer.

My father never had a day after my mom passed where he didn't drink. I worked and worked until I fell out in the fields and didn't get my share done. I opened my eyes to my father yelling at me to get up and get back to work. He had a whip in his hands, and he beat me nearly unconscious, all for being dehydrated. I almost died that day. When I got released from the hospital, my father picked me up. He started talking of the fields and the work that needed to be done that I had left when I decided to fall out like a wimp. He said a real man knows how to pace himself and not fall out like a missy. When my father was at a red light, running his mouth and looking at me like he had something planned for me back home, I jumped out. I ran and ran with him chasing in the truck. I hid out until he gave up searching for me. I woke up behind an outhouse and ran to the road. I hitchhiked my way to this town and I—

BJ: Travis, stop talking. I am looking at you. I am standing in the door. It's open. Come on in.

As Travis sits on the sofa, BJ makes them a pot of coffee. They talk and talk. When they look up, it is two o'clock in the morning. Travis is too tired to drive home. BJ offers to let Travis remain at her home and sleep in the spare bedroom.

Travis sleeps like a baby and doesn't want to wake. He never leaves the house. BJ gives him a new toothbrush. He washes, they eat breakfast, and they talk some more until everyone arrives for the meeting.

At the meeting, the plan is finalized. BJ will be the last young lady to take her mask off.

Quotes of Life

Appreciate you, live you, love you, and
it will help you appreciate others.

CHAPTER 28

KYLE AND TRICKY TEE

Kyle: Man, why are they always meeting up at his crib? I bet something is going down soon, and I want a part of it.

Tee: Man, shut up.

Kyle: You see Ms. BJ and Travis from that church up the street, and then there is Ms. Holier Than Thou Maria, Shay, and Dee Dee, all friends. Maybe they are having prayer to save the dyke. (Laughs.)

Tee: Man, you are a fool, Kyle.

Kyle: I know. Anyway, we have to meet the boys from uptown to make that switch and get back on our side of town. Man, why you say that J-Cob couldn't make it out? Man, he said something about a family emergency. Said his pops wanted them all to go and get his sister they never met. Say word!

Tee: Yes, word, dude. Now shut up.

Kyle: Man, I don't know, but every time lately we have to make a pickup, J-Cob is either with his pops or with some shortie on the other side of town. I just don't know about him sometimes. I think he is trying to back out. If so, I will give him one shot, but if he takes any money from this stash, he will be let out one way and that is in a bag.

Tee: Kyle, man, leave it alone and shut up, dude. You would not hurt a fly, man.

Kyle: Okay, then try me, Tee. Try me, dude, and you will see. I mean straight business, and I will get mine.

Tee: You need to stop using the product, and then I can see you on your feet, man. Now how much longer before we get there?

Kyle: We almost there, dude. Shut up and let me handle this like always.

Tee; Okay, but hey, did you ever get back with that other bone you were short last time on? You know these dudes are all about money.

Kyle: I know, Tee. Just drive and let it be, man.

Tee: I want to make sure we are straight; that is all.

Kyle: Man, you are always junking people, and someday you will pay. May just stop using, and then you will have enough money to pay for a new stash of good-good. Ya know what I mean, family?

Tee: I know, man, but what now?

Kyle. Man, there they go. And look, that is my man Todd from around the way.

Tee pulls in alongside Todd.

Todd: What up, boys? How is it going?

Kyle: Fine, my man, but where is Red? He was to be here to make the swap. I know he told me to be on time, and this fool is late.

Todd: Speaking of late, Kyle, you have been very late as of lately with Raul's funds. It is time to pay.

Kyle: Man, what you talking? Raul's not into this game like you think. Man we're out—

Todd pulls his gun.

Todd: Shut up!

Tee: Whoa! What's up? I am just driving, and you guys have me in some BS. I didn't come here for this, man, and I won't be handled like a punk.

Todd: I told your ass to shut up. Get out the car, punk. Move!

Tee moves to open the door, but slams the gas and pulls off with bullets flying. They cut the corner, and Tee is free to roll the hell out of that place. He looks over and sees Kyle bleeding from the head. He is gasping for breath. Tee knows he won't make it, but he tries to tell Kyle to hang on. They drive to Touro Hospital. Parking in front of the emergency room, Tee screams for help. Tee pulls Kyle from the car. He is completely distraught, since Kyle is now gone in his eyes. Kyle slips away slowly in Tee's arms. Tee vows revenge on Todd for killing his friend, and on Raul for sending Todd to make the hit.

CHAPTER 29

RAUL

Raul heads home from a night out with his boys. He finds Tee sitting on his steps, shirt covered in blood.

Raul: Man, what up? Are you okay?

Raul runs to Tee. Tee pulls a gun.

Tee: Stop right there, my man.

Raul: What up, tee? Why you tripping on me? I didn't do anything, man. You okay or something?

Tee: Man, you know what is up. Your hit failed, and it is time for you to pay.

Raul: Hit? Man, I know you are not serious.

Tee: Yeah, I am. Todd told me that you sent him to collect his funds.

Raul: Man, Todd? I have not talked to him since he was sent up for two years for some BS. You have got to be kidding me, man. I never would have sent anyone for you. Where is your boy Kyle?

Tee: Kyle is not here anymore, courtesy of you and your hit.

Raul: Man, you saying Kyle is gone?

Tee: Yes, man, he's gone, as you can see because I am wearing his blood. My man died in my arms an hour ago, and I came to see you personally. After I am done here, I am on the hunt for Todd.

Raul: Tee, look. It is not that way, man. I am not into drugs anymore. I am into the Lord. Man, please put that gun down and pray with me. I am not out here tripping anymore, Tee. I swear to you. Look. I will empty my pockets for you. I am not packing anything. I will never cross anyone's path again in a foul mode. Man, I went to Mia-Duke the other day, and I found myself in life. I gave that mess up a while ago. I was set free after I paid my bid to Big Pete. He let me out for two hundred grand, and I am out, man.

Tee: Then tell me why Todd would say your name and shoot at Kyle and me. We were picking up a stash for Big Pete and then got caught in the hail of fire. My man is gone because of some funny shit.

Raul: Tee, I know you are hurt and don't know who to believe. Pete would never hurt you or Kyle. Kyle may smoke some of the stash, but he always paid for his shit. Big Pete knew it and had no issue as long as Kyle was truly strung out.

Tee: Kyle was my boy, Raul.

Raul: And he was my brother.

Tee: What?

Raul: Yes. Kyle was my stepbrother.

Tee: I didn't know.

Raul: That is why I am telling you that I would have never put a hit out on my father's illegitimate child. Although I didn't let him know this, I still looked out for him. Together, you and I will make Todd pay. But he will pay with his life in prison. You and I are not killers. We are men of God, whether you believe it or not, and the Lord God will get him.

Tee: Man, what is wrong with you? You have really changed.

Raul: I have, and I will prove it daily. But first we have to get Todd while he still has that hot weapon. Where was he last seen?

Tee: Uptown, and I want him bad, Raul.

Raul: Don't worry, Tee. We will get him. I need to make a call. Come inside with me and we can get this going.

Raul calls Big Pete and tells him what happened. Big Pete delivers some information.

Big Pete: Yo, man. I am sorry about your little brother. I didn't know Todd would get out and come after you like this. And all for a girl you dated two years ago that he was loving.

Raul: Yes. He was feeling some chick named Dee Dee, but you came along and stirred that pot.

Big Pete: Man, I never touched that girl.

Raul: I know you didn't. But you had a thing for young girls, and Todd knew this.

Big Pete: Now when he was sent up, he heard of you and Maria. When he got out, he meant to pay you back and send you up so he could get with any girl you dated or loved.

Raul: Big Pete, you know where I could find him? Todd, that is.

Big Pete: He is still uptown, held up at his cousin G's house on Valance Street.

Raul: Cool, and I got you.

Big Pete: Raul, don't do anything stupid. I can have him ex-ex in thirty minutes.

Raul: Nah, I will not do anything. I will have his ass sent up for life this time. This will be his third time. Thank you for the information.

Raul and Tee drive to the location and place a call to the police, who are hot after the name Todd Morgan. At the door and surrounding the home, the police and SWAT team make their entrance. A shoot-out occurs. Todd takes a hit in the stomach and his cousin is killed on the spot for trying to shoot a cop who fell down.

Raul and Tee head home after a job well done and prepare for Kyle's send-off.

Todd lives and receives 220 years in prison with no chance for parole. He will die in prison, where he wronged so many inmates.

CHAPTER 30

JUDGMENT DAY

The day takes shape with all key players in position. There is an addition like no other, and she is flying like the sky. Nicole joins the party and makes sure they know she means business. Nicole became a part of the process by one day stopping by to check up on her girls. Hearing the knock on the door to BJ's home sent a shock wave to all inside and eventually ended up working out for everyone. Nicole plays the driver, and a sexy one. In order to get the girls there in style and to ensure that all is legit, Nicole will not only drive, but be known as a willing participant if the price is right. These brothers are loaded and willing to pay.

David: Okay, girls, listen up. Come on, y'all; it's time to get paid and bring these crumbs down, and I mean down. I have all in place. The house is bugged and cameras are all over, courtesy of my boys of course. So you will be in good hands. I have two SWAT team members in the attic, and they mean business. They are okay for the moment, being that that the home is cool, even in the attic. But still we have to make a move. Everybody gets restless, and I don't want them spoiling the fun for all of us.

BJ: Mom, don't worry. We will be okay.

Marcia: Baby, I know. It is just that I lost you once, and I can't lose you again. You are my world. I want so much for us.

BJ: That is true. Just think: with this payday, we will do just that. I want to be able to say they paid for their crime—not only financially, but physically. We could have asked to be quiet in life, but they would have sent someone to shut us up. Not today. We will shut them down and up for good, those nasty bastards.

The doorbell rings. BJ, opening the door, finds Grahams, Giselle, and Derek.

BJ: OMG! What are you all doing here?

Grahams: No, child. What are you doing dressed like that with these grown men in here? I want answers now, with my grandbaby in here and all.

David: Ma'am, if you would please come in, we can clear all this up. This is a sting operation, and your daughter has agreed to help out.

Giselle: Not my girl. She is only 16 and has not asked for my consent in any way. I won't have it. What if she were killed or hurt? OMG! Sir, what kind of system do we have when we let minors run the game?

Grahams, Sir, my baby girl needs to come home now. In fact all of these girls need to go home. I can't let them do such a thing, and I won't. It is too dangerous. Why are we using BJ, Shay, Dee Dee, Maria, and Nicole? All teenagers.

BJ: Ma'am, they are helping me to catch the men who raped me. I was used and used for their private gain. My mom and I will shut them down with the help of my friends.

Marcia comes out of the bathroom and stands looking at Grahams with a sad look of "I am sorry" on her face.

Marcia: Grahams, how are you? I know you are wondering what is up, but I am BJ's mother, and it is a long story that needs an ending.

Grahams: I know what that child told me, but I can't think of how she was used by you, her mother, while growing up.

Marcia: I sold my baby to those heathens for personal gain. Now we are trying to work it out with each other and stop them from hurting other families like mine. I was a fool for the dollar, and I lost my child because of that. If you want to take the girls and leave, it is okay. But BJ and I will go on with this and end it tonight.

Maria: Mom, Grahams, we have been working for a month to prepare. When I say working, I mean preparing for the takedown with the law on our side. We have everything worked out and in control. We just need to get there. It will be over before it even starts. The home is covered with cops all over, waiting to respond, and the nasty men don't carry weapons. They are millionaires who prey on young girls, and I want them put away. They are all over fifty now, so they will be old and crusty when they think of being released. They have to be stopped. We all agreed to help BJ do this. Mom, please. It has been worked out. The plan is so great. There is no way that anyone will be hurt. I need you on this one, Mother. I need you.

All the girls (coming forward, in unison): We are all in this together.

David: Ma'am. It will be okay. You can ride with the police in the security van and watch on camera as it all takes place. They have to be stopped, ma'am. They have to be, or someone else will be destroyed in life.

Giselle: Baby, are you sure you want to do this in the name of the law?

Maria: Yes, ma'am. I have to, BJ is my friend. It will be beneficial to us all. We will smile knowing they are locked up.

Giselle: Grahams, how do you feel?

Grahams: I feel like prayer … Everyone, please, come here and grab hands. Now please kneel with me. Let's pray for the protection of my babies under the law, but mainly in the name of my Father and the Lord Jesus Christ. Amen.

Nicole rises with a smirk on her face as she is dating Jesus. She laughs to herself, knowing the truth.

Giselle: Okay. The Lord has blessed us tonight. I want you to be safe, and we will be waiting for the word that you are all right. It won't be necessary to ride and witness this takedown in action. I won't be able to take it.

Grahams: Lord knows I won't. Let's get home, Giselle, and wait and pray. You girls have two hours or we will lose our minds.

CHAPTER 31

THE SECRET LOVERS

A cell phone rings.

Jesus: Hello? Oh hey, baby. How are you feeling?

Lakeeba: I am fine. I was just relaxing and thinking about you. I want to see you today.

Jesus: I know, right? Look, I can get over to the spot at three. You think you can make it, love?

Lakeeba: I know I can, but let me clear the way. My girls were expecting me at two, but I want to be held and not cracked on all day. I love them all, but a girl has got to do what a girl has to do sometimes, and that is ditch the bullshit and make it happen. I just need to know one thing.

Jesus: Yes, love?

Lakeeba: You and I have been kicking it quietly for about two months now. I want to know when we are going to make this public.

Jesus: You know I care for you. I am not sad at all about you and I being from different cultures. You know that you and I can be one, and no one has anything to say to this. But what about Paul and J-Cob?

Lakeeba What about them? They are my brothers and not the decision makers in my life. Listen, Jesus. I am in love with you. For a while now it has seemed as though I was the only one feeling this way. You admitted how you feel about me the other day, and now you are worrying about my newfound brothers. I had a life before them, and I will have one with them. So why are you hiding our relationship?

Jesus: Baby, we were going to tell the world, and then you up and said to hold on. I told my mother about you.

Lakeeba: My mother has put her home up for sale in Mississippi because it has so many sad memories. Now we are together, making things work here. She and I are really connecting and I want to be truly open with her. We have found a church and all. I am not leaving like I thought I was, and that is great. Now we can spend more time together and build on what we have. Jesus, tell me, is that the problem now?

Jesus: J-Cob has a secret, I know, and Paul has been upset with me for a while since I told him to watch his back when it came to my cousin Maria. I wanted them both to know that I mean business. I caught J-Cob, your brother, hugged up with Jo-Joan across town, and he was shocked as hell. He begged me not to tell, and I have not to this day. But now I sit here in love with his sister, and I am scared that he will do anything to protect his secret—and I mean anything. I know you guys just met and are trying to build as a family, but I am so scared because I crossed both your brothers one time in life. Paul is the quiet one, but he has a temper. J-Cob runs with Tricky Tee and Kyle, who are on Big Pete's payroll. I just don't want any problems. I love you, Lakeeba. I really do.

Lakeeba (laughing): Boy, is that it? Shut up and be quiet. I know about J-Cob's lifestyle.

Jesus: You do?

Lakeeba: Yes, and he let it be known. He has to just get himself together. He told Jo-Joan that it is over and to let him find himself in peace. It was deep that day, Jesus, but it was all for the best, and J-Cob is doing okay. Everybody is doing okay: my father, Mom, J-Cob, and Paul. Now as for Paul, he won't hurt you. In fact, I told him about us.

Jesus: What?

Lakeeba: Yes. Just last week to be exact. Paul had heard from one of his homeboys that you and I were spending a lot of quality time together. The dudes were joking about you becoming his brother-in-law one day.

Jesus: So what did he say?

Lakeeba: He said it was cool and you were an all right dude who causes no one any problems, works, and keeps to yourself most of the time. He said besides work, you and I were together every chance we got. He just asked me to be careful in life and not make any babies. (Laughs.)

Jesus: Oh, we won't. We both are not ready. But I am ready for one thing, Lakeeba …

Lakeeba: What is that, love?

Jesus: To tell the world that I love you.

Lakeeba: Oh, Jesus, you are so wonderful. I love you too …

CHAPTER 32

Judgment Continued

The limo approaches the house. The men sit patiently as their meals arrive in four pieces. Nicole parks in front of the home and steps out, looking oh so good. The men are looking out of a big window with the mouths open, waiting for the women to step out of the limo.

First, Dee Dee reveals a strong and sturdy leg decked out in clear crystal jewelry and looking fine. Next, Maria steps out in a lavish, knee-high Donna Karen getup that is pure beauty. Shay stands from her seat, covered from head to toe in a blue cashmere cat suit that hides nothing. Hidden behind masks, all three ladies create an atmosphere that is filled with passion. The men stand silent, unable to take a sip of their drinks.

The second butler, who is Travis, approaches with a tray full of ecstasy and the magical blue pill. He instructs them to take the blue pill and drink up. The men all take the blue pills and drink, never taking their eyes off the women.

The men's eyes widen beyond belief as *the one* stepped out of the car in a green, slick, body-hugging dress. Clustered jewelry sparkles for days, and a green mask hides her true beauty.

As the ladies stand and stare at the window, the maid and the butler gave one simple instruction: a new condom has to be used when entering a different girl. The blue pill will work its magic so that none of them will lose their manhoods. They are told that in thirty minutes, they will be given the ecstasy and led to the main room for an all-out unbelievable time. The men hungrily agree. Nicole makes her way to the front door to collect the money for three days of pure passion.

Met at the door by undercover agent Marline, a ten-year veteran, she is handed the bags that have been sitting on the front porch. Nicole counts the cases, which each contain one million dollars for a total of seven million. She can hardly keep her breath, but in the end maintains her composure.

When Nicole gives the nod, the men figure they have paid for four women but have got a bonus fifth girl. They smile from ear to ear.

The maid returns and tells them all is good and the four ladies will be up in a second. In the meantime, she tells them to relax, drink, and prepare to be out of breath all night. She smiles and walks off, looking so good that the men would have paid for her to join.

Agreeing, the men sip their drinks while the ladies are escorted to the door by Nicole and ushered in by the butler. Travis leads them to a room to relax and drink until it is show time. Nicole takes her time in bringing every suitcase to the car and loading them. Then she sips on a cold soda and waits, nervous as you know what, but with her girls inside looking so good and the place loaded with cops. The setup calls for one hour of mingling, and then the raid will begin.

Quotes of Life

Outer beauty uplifts us all, but inner beauty helps us survive. What do you possess?

CHAPTER 33

AUNT WILMA

While waiting for the raid to take place and their baby to return to them safely, Grahams and Giselle stand in the kitchen. Big Bo comes into the room after getting off the phone and goes the Grahams.

Big Bo: Grahams, I need for you to sit down, baby.

Grahams (sitting): What is wrong, baby? You ain't sick, are you? Lord, please no, not another situation. I thought we cleared everything up.

Big Bo: No, ma'am. Not quite everything.

Big Bo makes a quick call on his cell phone, and the doorbell rings a moment later.

Grahams: Who's at my door now? Lord, if it ain't one thing, it is another.

Giselle opens the door with a big smile on her face.

Giselle: Oh my Lord, if it ain't Aunt Wilma. Baby, I have not seen you in twenty-two years. I was just a teenager last time I saw you two. OMG! You look so wonderful. And Jimmy, how are you? Please come in. You both look so nice. We were having a family gathering, and nothing like more family coming to share in the love.

Grahams (scowling): Now why in the world are you two here? I know the Lord didn't just bless my family today only to scorn me right after the love expressed between everyone. I don't know why you are here, Wilma. The Lord has not spoken to me yet to forgive you. You hurt me. And you, Jimmy, how could you do what you did to me?

The family members are startled at what Grahams is saying and become concerned. They quietly listen.

Grahams: Jimmy, you took my heart and stepped on it. You treated me so bad, and all for what? I never did you wrong. I cared for you so much, Jimmy. I loved you with all my heart, and you go and run off with my stepsister? Oh God, help me here. Please God, walk with me ... (Crying:) Wilma, I gave you everything, and you had to take my man. Mom and Dad were so angry with you, and I told them that the Lord had spoken. You do deny me the chance to smile and be happy in life. How could you two do such a thing?

Wilma: Grahams, please listen. I tried to tell you from day one. I have tried and tried to reach you. Every time I got your number, you would change it; every time I mailed a letter, you would not answer it. I basically accepted the fact of you wanting nothing to do with me ever in life again. I gave you what you wanted, but Mia-Duke, I want my sister back. I need you. We need you.

Grahams: You need the Lord.

Jimmy: Grahams, can I speak, please? We didn't come all this way for nothing. We both hurt you and we both want to ask for your forgiveness in life. I know I led you on, but I always was in love with Wilma since high school. As it turned out, she wanted me too, but we were always with another person and not each other. I met you, Grahams, and I didn't know you two were sisters. I swear I didn't. When I started dating you, I ran into Wilma, and we talked and reminisced. I was wrong to date you and Wilma at the same time, but I was not married and wanted to know life, not be a whore out there. You were very sweet to me. You treated me like a real man should be treated. I never lay with you because I was sleeping with Wilma. I was drifting away into Wilma's arms, and I was too far gone to turn back the pages.

Grahams, you are a beautiful person and so special. But I was living a lie and had to come out with the truth. I couldn't lead you on, thinking we would be together. That is when I told you of Wilma, and you still had no idea. That day I told you to meet me at the park so I could be open with you. You were so beautiful and so happy, but I was hurting so bad because I needed the truth to be told. I got out of my car and you smiled. I went to the passenger's side of my car and opened the door, and Wilma got out. Your face became so distraught.

We had to let it come out that day. I never wanted to hurt you. I just couldn't get out the words to tell you I was in love with your sister. Grahams, it was meant to be. Wilma and I have been so happy in life. We have raised our kids together as one, hers from before our marriage and mine. Together we have six kids and ten grandchildren. Everyone is happy but Wilma, because she doesn't have you. Tulip talks now and then, but not you. You have disowned her, and for good reasons, but now is the time to stop and let us all be happy. I am sorry, Grahams, for what I done in the past. Please forgive me.

Wilma: My sister, I need you. I miss you (starts crying), and I can't go on smiling anymore without you, Grahams. I beg of you to please forgive me, forgive us, and accept our family as one. At the moment Jimmy and I took off twenty-two years ago, I was pregnant with your niece. Come here, Shantel. This is your aunt Grahams.

A beautiful young lady steps forward.

Shantel (in a country accent): Hello, ma'am. It is nice to finally meet you.

Everyone laughs.

Grahams: Come here, baby, and give Auntie a hug. (They hug.) It is nice to meet you also. I want you to go and mingle with you family members after I say this to my sister and brother-in-law. God doesn't like ugly; no, he doesn't. I have been very ugly to you, my sister, and you, Jimmy. I have held on to so much hate while trying to show much love to everyone. I want to beg for your forgiveness in life. I ask you to please open your arms, Wilma, and hug me and tell me you love me. (Crying.)

They move to each other, hug, and cry. There is not a dry eye in the home. Jimmy comes forward and hugs Grahams too, once again whispering he is sorry.

Grahams: I forgive you. Please continue to take care of this family. But please, we need for everyone to sit and relax. I will of course talk to you all, but we are waiting for an important call from a very important situation. I hope you all don't mind if Giselle and I head to the back to wait by the phone. Thank you all.

CHAPTER 34

JUDGMENT CONTINUED 2

Mr. Tom Wills, Mr. Jake Seamier, Mr. Samuel Miller, Mr. Robert Thompson, Mr. Gregory August (which rings a bell with BJ because he always asked for her every two days), Derrick Jones, and Bobby Matthews are completely horny and ready to feast on their prey. The men begin to discuss damaging events that have occurred over the years.

Gregory: Man, I think this is going to be better than anything we have ever done as a group. I mean, you seen them all.

Bobby: They are all young, sexy, and I know beautiful under those masks.

Gregory: Yeah, I know, and I didn't pay a million to look at a mask. I want to lick a face as I do my thing. It will be what we want, as Marcia stated.

Tom: By the way, did any of you hear from her?

Derrick: Nah, man. She is keeping it quiet until the girls return with her money. She says she is all about business and didn't want to walk in here and steal our attention away from the young girls. She still can handle her business. (Laughs.)

Samuel: Yeah, right. Have you seen Marcia lately? I wouldn't want her in any way. This young stuff next to that used goody is not any comparison.

Jake: Please fellas, let's not worry about that old shit. Let's get our drink on, man up, and attack our feast. And I don't anyone of you panting when you're talking about OMG! I can't take it. We may be in our fifties, but we will send these young things back home hurting, crying, paining, and never wanting to see us again. Like that … umm … what's her name? Marcia's daughter? What is her name?

Rob: You and Tom couldn't get enough of that young one.

Tom: She was called BJ, and her name was Brittany. I won't forget the things I did to her and the way she cried, begging for her mom, who never came. I kind of felt bad, but hey, I paid. Right, fellas? Shit, we all paid for any and everything we screwed. The younger they were, the better.

Gregory: Yeah. But one thing I know we better not have done, and that was hurt a girl under fifteen. I was not for that. You bastards better not have messed with anyone under fifteen or there will be talk.

Bobby stays real quiet because he is a straight pervert and will screw anyone. He is the foulest one of the group, but he is rich.

The maid Marline has served the men drinks for nearly thirty-five minutes. She's fed them knickknacks to build their stamina and sex drive for the night. During their wait, the men incriminate themselves in nearly a dozen cases of sexually assaulting eighteen different young girls. Parents have filed complaints over the years, but the police never found enough evidence to convict. Now their plate of evidence is full. They can take the nasty boys at any moment, but the more evidence, the merrier. Life is great for Detective David Dickens. These animals will soon be behind bars for life, rich or no rich.

Marline: Okay, gentlemen, if you would please proceed to the main bedrooms. Take a shower and freshen up. You would not want these beautiful young ladies putting their tongues on something foul, would you? There are robes in every room, and cologne. Please feel free and make it right. I advise you not to touch yourselves, as you may be joined in the shower or may not. Just don't mess up what's to come in, let's say, twenty minutes. See you then.

The men take off to the many rooms and prepare.

The signal is given. Detective Dickens and his boys come into the home, let in by the first butler, who is also a detective. He leads them to the basement to wait for the breaking of a glass, which is the signal for their bust to happen.

The men all get themselves together and head to the main foyer, waiting for the first girl to appear. But instead of one girl, three walk in. They are all in beautiful lingerie and looking oh so tasty. They remove their masks and, one by one, lick their lips and stare at the men. The men are already hard, ready to penetrate a horse if they are not released soon.

But as they are about to take a step to the young women, the fourth young tender steps into the room, wearing a thong. She has short hair, beautiful breasts, and legs to die for. She is absolutely stunning even with her mask on. She nods to Maria, Maria nods to Shay, and Shay nods to Dee Dee. The men get the notion that this tender is the leader, and feel that they are in for a night of unbelievable fun.

The young tender makes the move to remove her mask and reveal her face. Shay picks up a glass of wine and throws it to the wall, shattering crystal all over the wall. The men get excited. The signal has been given, and the detectives stand behind them, watching for the next move. The SWAT team enters from upstairs. The front door open, and more enter cops with guns undrawn. This is to be a quiet capture …

The men are startled at the sudden appearance of the cops. They immediately start to plead their cases. Marcia walks in.

Marcia: Hello, Derrick. Nice to see you here, and your goons. I just wanted you to know that I followed you tonight, knowing you were up to no good as you have always been. Look at you now, about to use more young ladies like you used me and my daughter for your sick pleasures. But you won't hurt these young ladies and won't ever hurt me again in life.

While Marcia is talking, three of the girls have grabbed their things. They are ushered out of the house and into the waiting limo with Nicole. The fourth girl, BJ, remains, looking at Tom and Bobby and Gregory with strained eyes behind her mask. She wants to kill them on the spot. Her mother knows this and motions for David to go to her, because she is about to do something wrong.

Reaching over to the couch, BJ grabs for a gun. She points it at the scared men, who are wondering why they are about to be shot.

Tom: Wait! Wait! Young lady, what are you doing? We have not touched you girls, so why are you pointing that gun at us? Please stop and put it down.

Bobby: Please put it down, young lady.

All the men stand and wait for the young lady to react to the request.

Marcia: Baby, we got them. Please put it down.

Tom: Baby? you called her baby? Marcia, is that BJ?

Gregory: Nah. Can't be. She ran away after we—

Samuel: Shut up, fool!

Gregory: Why should we? If it is her, so be it. We are all done. She might as well end my misery, because I will suffer behind bars and in life.

BJ removes her mask. The men stare at the most beautiful young lady they have ever seen. They say they are sorry and for her to please not hurt them. They beg and beg. BJ lowers the gun, which is taken by David. Marcia grabs her baby and walks toward the door, vowing to sit every day in court to watch the men being taken down.

CHAPTER 35

LIMO RIDE TO FREEDOM

BJ, crying, climbs into the limo with four other frightened young ladies, all tired and ready to get out of Dodge. Nicole, too nervous to drive, takes a sip of the brandy she took from the house as she ran to help the girls down the steps in their high heels. She tells everyone to hold on. David stands next to the car, smiling. He knows a payday has come for the service of the five young, beautiful ladies, and he will collect for all who helped out in the raid.

The money exchange was not caught on camera. The bags were taken to the porch. The camera only captured the bags leaving the main room. Therefore, any claim of a funds transaction cannot be proven. Simple and clever.

The girls drive across town and enter a garage. A van is parked there for them to make a switch.

Waiting next to the van is Mark, David's brother. He knows the deal and does what he's been instructed. He retrieves two cases containing a million dollars each and drives off never looking back. The girls get in the van and drive off. The limo is picked up the next day with $1,000 sitting on the seat for the owner, David's sister's husband, Michael.

Maria, having been gone over an hour, places a call to Grahams and Giselle, letting them know all is good and she should be home soon.

Grahams: I am so proud of you, baby. But never, and I say *never*, let this happen again. You heard me, child. You making my blood pressure rise, all in the name of the law. Help me, Lord! Now when will you be home?

Maria: In about thirty minutes. I have to get my things from BJ, and I am on my way. Love you, Grahams.

The girls come to the projects, where a car is waiting. They jump in with the remaining suitcases and are driven to the next destination across town. There they switch to Shay's SUV, get in with the cases, and drive off again. The car is left for the owner, a cousin of David's, again with $1,000 under the seat. All is worked out and under control.

The girls meet again at BJ's home. All the players gather to drink sodas and close the situation.

David: Okay now, girls, we did it. Thank you.

Marcia: Yes, thank you.

BJ (crying and looking at her mother): Mom, I love you.

Marcia: I love you also.

The girls talk to David, who informs them that the men claim money was exchanged, but that there are no signs of cash anywhere.

David: The cameras showed the backs of you girls when you removed your masks. We took four girls who fit your descriptions to court and they played their role, of course being paid for the acting. They denied ever having any contact with the men or any knowledge of money. They were young ladies who were prostitutes back in the day. They got paid and went on their way. Being minors, they were returned to their homes, financially smiling, with their parents knowing only that they ran away.

Dave prepares to leave. He is sent on his way with hugs. Smiles are spread across everyone's faces. "Thank you" is all that is heard for a moment.

David: Take care, everyone. BJ, I am glad you got justice. I am sorry for not catching assholes like this earlier in life. I am sorry.

BJ: Mr. David, I thank you again. You don't know how much this means to me and my mother. I need to focus on us, and that is what I will do. The Lord will be a part of this process. I thank you again, and take care.

The doorbell rings. Travis is standing at the door, looking oh so good.

Travis: BJ, how are you?

BJ (smiling): Hi, Travis. I am fine. Oh please, I am sorry. Please come in. Place your jacket on the chair and come sit down. All are here talking.

David: Hi, Travis. I have to be out, but please take care of BJ.

Shay: What? I mean, what he say, BJ?

BJ: He said for Travis to take care of me.

Shay: Oh. I thought he said that.

BJ: Shay, can I talk to you in my room for a second, please.

Shay: Sure.

BJ: Look, girl, what is your problem?

Shay: BJ, why is he here? I thought you told me you needed time to find you.

BJ: I told you to let it go, Shay. I am not gay as I lived. I lived a lie. I need to move on. Travis is a cool guy and you know it. Please let me go. Please. I am sorry for the love that was created between us, but I want a man in my life. I think he is the one, girl. (Crying:) Shay, please. I do love you, but we have to move on and not live this lie. It's not right with me and probably ain't right with God. I need to be me and not what you want me to be.

Shay: I know, girl, and I am with Tim. But I find myself thinking of you. Why is that?

BJ: Because we had a love affair and it just doesn't leave like that. But you can't have your cake and want ice cream. I don't want the ice cream, Shay. I want only cake, and Travis is so nice. Okay? Now can we try to move on, chick?

Shay: Yes, BJ. I will try hard, and I mean hard, but I do miss your touch, girl. You know you were wrong for what you did, but I guess Travis can see why I am so crazy for you. I love you, chick. I love you …

Maria: About time you finish that secret-crap talking. If I am not in, don't let it happen again, and I mean it, girls. Got Travis in here looking all good and stuff. I might forget I love Paul and attack. Just playing, BJ—I see that "I will kick your ass" look on your face.

BJ: Okay now, everyone. Time to wrap it up. I have company. That means you too, Mom. I love you all, but you have got to go. And I mean now. Wait one moment, Travis …

Everyone says good-bye to Travis with only Shay sounding distant. But she knows it is for the good of friendship.

CHAPTER 36

THE COURT VERDICT

The trial is long and drawn out. The media is out in force. Celebrities make their appearance in support of the nasty men, not knowing if the verdict and the truth will hurt their careers or help them.

There are big names, since the men funded movies for the stars. The witnesses for the state are on key and paid. The men, who can't tell shim from shine, only know there were beautiful ladies in makeup with beautiful skins and shapes. The blue pill and the lack of sex played their part, as did the ecstasy and their vision blurred with alcohol. It was a pretty setup. The camera never caught any drugs, and the defense had nothing to present as evidence. Of course the men's systems did show drugs, but no one could say they didn't take drugs on their own as a part of the sexual escapade.

Frustrated with the lack of evidence, the defense tries to delay the trial. The defense lawyers are fired, but the new set of players to the game can do no more. It turns out that this case broke the backs of many who were involved from state to state. In all, sixty-two people are arrested.

The perverts stand tall at the beginning of the court session and even smirk at the judge to let him know that this is a no-brainer.

Clerk: Mr. Tom Wills, would you please take the stand. Please place your right hand on the Bible and raise you left. Do you swear to tell the truth, the whole truth, and nothing but the truth, so help you God?

Tom: I do.

Detective David Dickens sits and wonders how many times he's seen people lie right there in court with their hands on the Bible, swearing to tell the truth in the name of the Lord. People are unbelievable and will lie for anything. The detective waited for the juice to be poured thick. Then it comes in a thunderstorm.

Prosecutor: Sir, did you or did you not have sex with underage girls?

Tom: I had sex with females, sir. I would consider them all over the legal age limit.

Prosecutor: Sir, so you are telling the court the truth, as you have sworn to do so. You are saying that you had no knowledge of the girls being under the age of eighteen. Right, sir?

Defense: Objection, your honor.

Judge: Denied. I want to hear his answer.

Tom: Sir, I said that I thought they were of age. If a girl was younger than that, then I had no knowledge.

Prosecutor: Sir, did you pay women with daughters to have sex with their kids?

Out of nowhere, Tom starts saying one phrase over and over, suddenly irate: "I plead the Fifth! I plead the Fifth!" His lawyer is shocked and calls for the court to be adjourned for fifteen minutes so he can speak to his client.

Defense (in a side bar): Mr. Wills, what seems to be the problem? You are going against everything I went over with you. What are you doing?

Tom: Look, they have our asses, and I will do whatever it takes to save my skin. At least I will be able to see the light of day one day. Now let me be. I want off the stand. I have no chance to win. I will take their asses under with me if they don't do the same.

After about an hour of the Fifth being pleaded, the prosecutor states he has no more questions, and the defense says the same.

Clerk: Mr. Bobby Matthews, please take the stand.

He is sworn in.

Prosecutor: Sir, can you state your name?

Bobby: Bobby Green Matthews.

Prosecutor: Sir, can you tell the court where you were on the night in question?

Bobby: I was at a party where a few beautiful young ladies showed up, ready to attack. And I being a man, wanted to play.

Prosecutor: So are you not married?

Bobby: I am, and I admit doing wrong, but I didn't have sex with any young girls that day or back on the nineteenth of August, as you have listed there, sir. I was at home. And if they tried to put me there, I didn't know anything of her being beaten that way, and that tattoo was not real. So don't play me on this stand.

The court room sits silent as the raving comes to a halt.

Prosecutor: Sir, I don't know what you are talking about. I think we need to look into this case you are speaking of. But since you sliced the cake—what happened to that girl?

Bobby (crying:): I plead the Fifth. I plead the Fifth. Get me off this stand. I plead the Fifth.

Bobby has a nervous breakdown right there on the stand. An ambulance has to come and take him to the ward.

One by one the men come to the stand, and one by one they incriminate themselves in their own cases and give details of other cases. They all thought their money and power could buy them freedom. They all plead the Fifth after fighting for days and months. They are simply jokes, and the judge tires of them. But he is really angry at Bobby Mathews, because Bobby, on tape at the house, had described some similar activity that had happened to someone the judge knew. The judge wants to find out why.

The men try to claim that they were all set up. They pay incredible sums of money to dream-team lawyers, only to be found guilty. They each receive seventy-five years in prison with no chance of parole. The sentences are a reduction from 125 years for their cooperation in bringing down more nasty men. Witnesses come forward from everywhere, making this the case of the century in New Orleans. The men of course cry, and their wives, children, and grandchildren cry, just like the young girls cried when they begged for the nasty men to get off of them and let them go to their mommies.

The judge is not lenient, since his daughter has been attacked by a nasty man in the past. The judge has vowed to fight to the death to bring them all down. Of course, when the defense learns the judge's life story, they try to have him dismissed, but the city will not have it. He does a marvelous job all the way to the end. He cries when the verdict is read as he thinks of his daughter, who was found beaten nearly to the death.

Something tells him that Bobby was involved. He ends up ordering a DNA test that proves valuable, showing a direct match. He almost jumps off the bench when the results are made public.

Bobby receives a sentence of 278 years for his actions in life. He is to become real bait for the perverts in prison. No one cares, not even his wife, who divorces him as soon as he enters prison.

Many of the mothers who sold their kids for cash end up losing their kids for life. Marcia and BJ find some kind of solace with the million dollars to help in building their relationship.

The nasty boys' financial empires are sued for nearly everything, only leaving enough for their wives to live on. The companies are turned over to the victims, who sell everything and split the amount equally among all sixty-two women. BJ ends up owning a major company on her own, but she sells it for only half its worth. She wants nothing to remind her of the men who violated her. But she now possesses enough money to live a happy life.

CHAPTER 37

SHAY

Shay can't get over the fact of BJ and Travis making things happen for them in the way they have. She is truly in love with a young lady who has clearly stated that she has no time for a woman again in her life. BJ wants to live as a full-grown woman, respect life, get married, and have kids. Shay is disgruntled and wants nothing but to break up BJ's happiness in an attempt to bring BJ back to being lesbian. BJ is having none of it.

Shay plots and plans and fakes it so hard in the presence of Travis that he thinks it is a trip how nice she is to him. Travis even takes it as a sign to keep his distance, so BJ will not think he wants her friend. Travis is a good man and does so much to ensure BJ knows that he loves her. Their love has never been tested in any way, but now BJ has to deal with a former sex partner. Shay had it all and wants more, but no matter how much pressure she puts on them, BJ will not give in to her antics.

Shay's relationship with Tim doesn't last long. She tries hard to move on, coming to a block each time with thoughts of BJ, until one day she meets Charles Drake. He is a nice and happy young man who has dreams. He is from a wealthy upstate family. Charles is a senior in college and very popular with the ladies. But he is popular only by looks, as he has never given in or taken advantage of anyone. He is a good man, and Shay knows it. She only has to move on from BJ completely, but can she?

Shay knows she has to stop loving BJ so hard. But she also knows that if Charles finds out she lived a lie sexually in the eyes of many, he might not want to be with her. She has to keep his focus on her and not on her past with another woman. No matter how much Shay misses the touch of BJ, she has never gone to another female. She always remains with a guy to keep her focus. But how can she let herself go and take a real chance on a charming young man?

Shay is a beautiful young lady, and Charles is a handsome fellow. Charles knows of his good looks, but he is very modest and certainly not interested in bragging on himself, as many good-looking men do in this world. Charles knows that Shay has to be chased, and he is not into the business of running down many women. He doesn't want it to be an issue in life to want and not have. Shay does, however, convince herself to give Charles a chance and date him for him and only him.

Charles is the man and Shay's new man. To many, they are a cute couple. Shay is not a virgin, and Charles knows that the day will soon come when they will experience the sweeter side of their life together by making love. Three months after dating and feeling each other out, the day arrives—and what a day it will be. Charles goes all out to prove that he is the man of all men, and the man who can give her more than a financial smile on her face.

The Marriott Hotel, downtown Bourbon Street. Roses lie all over the room. The setting is more beautiful that eyes can imagine. His theme for the night is clear. Shay's eyes are fixed on the marble floors and rose petals that lead to the bedroom "OMG!" is all she can say in anticipation of their feast for the evening. She knew that the extra time she spent in her bathroom preparing for this day would be worth it. She can't wait to have him in her arms.

Charles: So I see you like the scenery.

Charles comes up from behind Shay, who is taking in the view of the entire room and the balcony, which she knows will play its part in the night.

Shay: I do, and I must say that you have gone way above my expectations. I guess you must really want me in such a special way.

Charles: Oh how much. You don't know. I want the moment to be right and on point. I know, as we have talked about it, that we are both not virgins, but who cares about the past? It is about you and I from this point on, and I must do what I know to provide unlimited pleasure to your beautiful frame. And oh, how beautiful you are to me daily. This moment will be etched in my mind forever, love.

Hearing Charles call her "love" startles Shay, yet brings a calmness to her heart. She didn't want to give her all to just a friend. Knowing that he has love in his heart is relaxing, so relaxing that she asks him to repeat his last word. He takes a sip of his Crown and Coke.

Charles: I love you, Shay.

He brings her closer to him and plants a soft kiss on her luscious lips.

Shay: Umm so tasty.

She applies an even more passionate kiss to his soft lips. Shay knows that she is in trouble. His lips are soon to pleasure her in her most sensitive spots that only a few have had the chance to see, touch, and taste. She wants him badly and they both know it. They play it off and enjoy their time together. They have cleared two days away from family, college, and friends, all to be together in the most passionate way known in life.

They laugh and eat room service while sneaking a touch now and then, as well as frequent kisses. They know the deal. It includes passion, straight passion. As they finish eating, there is a tear in Shay's eyes. She has never in her life been treated with such love, calmness, passion, and respect by any man she has ever known, including family.

Startled by a touch from Shay, Charles regains composure. As he moves in to kiss her yet again, she smiles. She is completely shaking in her bones for this man's touch. Charles nearly collapses from the touch of her pure, soft hands. His teeth are grinding. His palms are sweating. Trying to hold out, Charles turns to face the balcony as he applies sweet kisses to her neck. Shay backs away, having reached the point of fainting. Charles lays his beautiful Shay to the floor and mounts her. He kisses and caresses and strokes her body. She is his.

Looking up, Charles sees the balcony. He has never had the pleasure of taking a woman on one. He stops kissing Shay and lifts her and guides her straight to the place where he will have a taste of her sweet juices for the first time.

He wants her on the balcony rail, her feet spread as he takes his love to another place, a place called passion. Looking straight to the sky, he imagines what's next: pure pleasure and an emotional ride of disbelief. He presses his lips to her back.

Charles: Now Shay, I want you to do as I say. It will be sweet and painless.

Shay agrees, knowing in a way what is next.

Charles: Turn around let me work the other side. In about forty seconds, I want you to turn once again.

He glides his hands up and down her legs, wanting her to relax. He is also nervous as hell.

Charles: I am not finished. You will know it when I fill you with my manhood, but not now, love. I am hungry, and I am a man who likes to eat.

He begins to kiss Shay's back again. He becomes mesmerized by her beautiful body, which smells so sweet. He needs to touch her more. He needs to taste her. He needs to have her now. And now is what happens. They smile at each other as she looks back and sees him admiring her beautiful behind. He slowly presses his lips softly on her buttocks. From there he tastes, bites, sucks, and drowns in her fluids. She has now come at least four times and is barely holding on to the railing. Shay's hands are shaking and beginning to hurt.

Shay can't take it anymore. She knows what to do. She spins around, shocking Charles, and brings him up to kiss her. From there it is on. She kneels and removes Charles's pants. She stares in amazement at his size, knowing she has struck gold. And a person never lets go of gold unless in need. She has to have a taste, and taste she does, letting him know he has a woman who can handle her own.

Charles and Shay take each other on the balcony for two hours. The breeze picks up and they both need a break. They bring it inside to the bedroom, where their attacks continue and never let up for two days.

Disgruntled (A Description of Pain)

Distant, alone, cold and dark
Not everyone experiences the true grit of emotions
Maybe one can identify, but the true
one has the notion of knowing
Why have I become so angered with society?

My happiness is hidden within my own recognizance
Awakened by needs to respond openly
To talk, to reason, to think
But never to compromise
See, that would just make one classified as crazy
And I, for one, am not losing my
mind or chain of thoughts
I am just sad …
But as distant as I am, I am still focused
Focused for the wrong reasons
Hell, I am further away from reasoning
than one might think
But yet I am living in an unspoken manner
Compliments mean nothing with reason
And reasons are what are given for my senseless actions

You know, to me, praises are a mere
form of childish handouts
Examples of a mode to travel for worthless wealth
And a ride for accomplishing the thoughts of truth
Truth that mean absolutely nothing to me because
I am sad …

See, people take me for granted, and I see
individuals for what they really are
Trash that doesn't register against me
People who are not able to stand side by side and smile
People who laugh at silly jokes or
one who looks for something
Even if something is really nothing
You may say that you don't think of yourself
But it is you who are self-centered and distant
I compliment myself, I praise
myself, and I answer myself
And damn it, I believe in myself
Truly, I am never wrong

But to be frank
I am disgruntled
I am disgruntled
I am disgruntled
Simply put.
I am sad …

Quotes of Life

The sky is only high if your goals are unreachable.

CHAPTER 38

Two Years Later

At Charity Hospital, in the intensive care unit, where patients who are hanging on to life by way of comas rest peacefully, Kyle has somehow survived his deadly wound. He has been placed in a coma to relieve the swelling on his brain. It has been some time since the shooting. The doctors have basically written him off and will soon pull the plug if family members don't claim him soon.

After a deep and intense meeting, the doctors determine that it is no longer useful to have Kyle suffer any longer in his state. The swelling has reappeared out of nowhere and triggered a reaction never seen. Kyle shakes violently as if he is trying to wake but is being held back by something. It seems to end with him losing; he stops shaking and goes back to his quiet state as if nothing ever happened.

A doctor enters the room where Kyle lies. A priest is there to deliver the last rites. Kyle's eyes are suddenly wide open. He is trying to speak.

"What in the world! Oh my God, he is awake and breathing normally," the doctor says. Kyle indeed is awake and breathing normally. He seems to want to ask a question. The doctor moves closer to hear what Kyle is trying to say. He removes the tubes running in Kyle's nose and mouth to let him breathe on his own. When one of the nurses tries to stop him, the doctor states loudly that Kyle is okay and let it be. He continues to work. As soon as the tubes are removed, Kyle speaks quietly and freely, saying one name: "Todd …"

Kyle is moved to a recovery room. He is taught motor skills and learns to speak once again without any issues. Of course he will require work on the scar that he now has to live with. But the bullet only pierced a slight part of his brain, enough to knock him out and make it seem as if he were dead.

Tee, not knowing any CPR, assumed Kyle was dead and told everyone so. If Tee had only taken the classes that were offered to him and his friends, he would have known and been there for Kyle. But in the end, Kyle had to suffer alone without any family members laying claim to him.

Kyle ends up recovering. He is able to function and get on his feet. But Kyle has been moved four states over so that doctors can study his progress and try to work their magic to bring him back to life. Kyle is now living in Chicago, alone. He is not financially fit to make moves and has to work hard to earn enough money to make it back to New Orleans and the only friends he has in life.

Kyle becomes clean and sober and really begins to strive in life. He becomes known to his workmates at Walmart as a go-getter, a hard charger, and a no-nonsense manager who will fire you in a minute if you don't perform up to his expectations. Kyle is truly becoming a man in life.

Kyle eventually catches the eye of a nice-looking young lady who is on her way to becoming someone in life. She is a paralegal for a well-known firm in Chicago and is on her way up. Her name is Brianna James. She is strong in life and means business.

As Kyle looks to improve his status in life, he enrolls in college and takes classes. He earns an AS degree in business. Kyle is truly proving himself. He wants so badly to show his friends that he has changed, but he is not ready. There is more that he has to accomplish. He knows where it started, and that is church. Having dated Brianna now for two months, Kyle attends Brianna's church and begins to get the words of wisdom and guidance he has been seeking. He becomes a member of her congregation, active in church and blossoming into a junior deacon.

Brianna and Kyle date for about a year. Kyle is now a paralegal in her law firm, and Brianna is a full-time lawyer. Kyle knows it is time to ask her that beautiful question about her becoming his wife. Kyle's scar is healed and covered with his own hair growth when he marries Brianna in a beautiful wedding fit for the stars to see. One thing missing: his friends. But Kyle figures he has moved on in life. There is no way he will return to the drugs that ate away at his system for years.

At the wedding, Brianna, looking into Kyle's eyes, gives him the news of the decade. He is brought to tears when she tells him she is two months pregnant. Kyle and Brianna will go on to start a beautiful life and purchase a new home. They have a baby girl and name her Kylie. She is precious, the most beautiful young baby you could lay eyes on.

Kyle is truly living his life and leaving the bullshit behind. He and Brianna are a match made by God. Kyle becomes a full-time deacon and a mentor to many who are living or have lived in his shoes. He is a great man. It is evident in how far he has come in life. Being given a second, third, and maybe even a sixth chance to live a life, he is truly thankful to God. He prays every night, thanking God for allowing him to see the light, meet Brianna, and have a beautiful young daughter.

Kyle knows that one day he will see his old life eye to eye. He wants so badly to put that to sleep and move on. It is not the drugs that Kyle is scared of; it is the fact of seeing his friends still suffering in life, on drugs and in gangs. There is no need to feel peer pressure coming in his direction. He is as strong as ever and has God, Brianna, and Kylie on his side. He just doesn't know when or where that meeting will take place. But it will come soon enough.

CHAPTER 39

MARIE (20) AND RISING

Marie: Hi, Mom. What's up?

Giselle: Nothing, baby. I was just checking in on you. I have not heard from you in a while, and I wanted to hear my baby's voice.

Maria: I am sorry. I have been rolling here and there, but I am okay. I think of you more and more and more each minute I am away from you and Grahams. I miss you, Mom.

Giselle: I miss you also, baby. Now I don't want to worry you, but I want you to come and see your grandmother more. She is getting up there and one day won't be here for us all as a family.

Maria: What? Mom, is Grahams okay? I don't want my granny to die, Mom! (Cries.)

Giselle: No, love; she is okay. I just think of her every minute. You and I want us all to know her in this lively stage. Then, when she gets up there, I want you to be able to remember and talk of the times you were in her heart and soul early on.

Maria: Okay. I will get home today to see my granny and you. I don't want anything happening to you all. I need you to be by my side. I am so happy to have parents like you. I am so in awe when it comes to what you two have done in life. I have been blessed in so many ways, and it will continue, Mom. I am now taking drama classes and singing in numerous events. I want to do something different in the family, and I think I can make it big. I don't want the issues, and I won't have them, because I have funds coming in soon. I won't be on anyone's casting couch. I want to make it on my own and not with any false help in life. I got the Lord, Grahams, and you. I will make this happen for me as soon as I graduate.

Giselle: Baby, I am so glad of your choice to remain in college and get your degree before you venture out on your own. I want the best for you, and you are giving the best to us all. But what of Paul, baby girl?

Maria: Paul is cool, but I don't think he wants me to venture away from him too far. He has plans to marry me one day, but I don't want to be married and have kids now. I want to live my life. This is not the early days. No disrespect, but I want life. I must do this my way and not with a man to challenge my ways. I am not out there. I love Paul and don't want him to go to another woman. But I also want him to be there for me. I want to date him and move up in life with him. But it has to be on both our terms. I don't think that this is the time to reverse my plans in life. I think this is the time to support me and support my choices as I support his. Mom, I do think he is a little bothered about my choice to work and not let him takes care of me. I don't need that; I need for us to be one and in accord. I know this sound like it is all about me, and it is in a way, but I have plans to do things and not remain in New Orleans for a long period of time. I want to do what I want with his blessing.

Giselle: Maria, although I want you to be with Paul and marry one day, I understand your drive. I had the same drive and determination. Then I made the choice to have sex and have you. I am so proud of you, and I have been for my entire life. Now you have been a headache many times, but then again, you have grown into the woman you are today, and I stand a proud mother. Thank you for turning out the way you did. But let no danger enter your life without the Lord to guide you through. Always believe in the Lord, and it will come as one.

Maria: As a junior in college, there is so much for me to do and always something going on to challenges my thought pattern. You have to remain in charge of your life or you will fall as well as fail. What do you want in life besides a headache? I want to smile and be happy.

But get this: there are so many hot guys out there … OMG! And Paul knows it. That is why he wants to lock me down and take me off the market. I keep telling him my choice is him, but he still acts nervous at times. I want him to know that I got me and I won't put myself in any bad situations.

A girl name Brandi Jones came up pregnant the other day. She doesn't know who the father is. She was deemed "the recruiter girl." She would show new college players around daily when they came to campus, and whatever would happen. Now she doesn't know who the daddy may be, a white guy or a black guy. It is a shame before God. At least her dumb self will have some type of financial support if that player makes it big. But you know that all who slept with her will try to convince her to abort, and I don't think she will go for that. Now the school is on trial, because if she opens up, all hell will break loose. A lot of people want to pay her off, but she is not killing her child and they know it. I am glad I am not in her shoes. I have remained truthful to Paul.

I know there is a lot out there, but there is also a lot to catch out there besides an unwanted child. I won't be that person in life. I will be that responsible young lady with merits. I live for my God, Mom.

Giselle: OMG! Oh Lord, I am so proud of you, love. You have really grown. I am on cloud nine, love. Baby, I will see you soon. Please stay safe and on point. I need to hear you at church one Sunday, okay, love?

Maria: Okay, Mom. Please take care and we will talk later.

CHAPTER 40

JO-JOAN

Jo-Joan has moved on with another man. D is how he likes to be referred to by Jo-Joan. Their relationship has been a secret for two years.

Jo-Joan: Hello, D. What's good? Why you been slipping the past few days? You and I have become a serious item, and I don't think I can handle this separation you keep trying to pull.

D: Man, look, you know we have to keep this on the low. If my family finds out I am punking it on the side, they will lose their minds.

Jo-Joan: First of all, don't call me "man." I am a woman, and you know it. That is why you can't stay away from me. You know the deal, boo, so stop tripping!

D: I see you have jokes now, but truly, why you keep pressuring me like this? I spend damn near three days a week in your bed, and that is not enough?

Jo-Joan: Hell, nah, it ain't enough. I want you with me every day. I felt for J-Cob and was hurt in the end. Now, after two years of sneaking around with you, it's like I have found myself again. I won't lose out this time, I promise!

D: There you go again, ranting and raving about not losing again. Listen, Jo-Joan, I am not for being put out on front street. If you can't understand that, then you have not been listening at all.

Jo-Joan: Listen yourself, D. Stop hiding the truth. Hell, you came to me and not me to you.

D: Nah. I came to see what you were so broke up about that day in the jazz hall. You were so sad, and I felt a need to comfort you in some way. I didn't think we would be this close, but we are. I am with you, but I told you then and I will tell you now: it is a side thing. I truly feel that I am not gay. I simply wanted to see what the whole world was mad about in two people of the same sex having a sexual relationship.

Jo-Joan: And so you think you can just travel over to Gayville and then head back home to Straightville? Nah, pimp, it ain't that easy when you build feelings for someone. D, I have fallen in love with you on a level you know. I have been nothing but faithful to you and even allowed you to dabble back and forth with that fish-hideout girl of yours. But every time I see her out, I want to smash her in the face for being a part of my man's life that I allowed.

D: Jo-Joan, if you choose to be violent in the world, then that is when I need to split. I can't have you tripping and going off on people because we have a side thing.

Jo-Joan: Nah, D. We have a relationship, and you know it. I am just a woman who lets you get out from time to time to fill a void. But in the end I know I will have you all to myself. Have your fun for now, but just wait and see. Jo-Joan gets what she wants in life, and my life has you in it from here on out. Trust me, boo.

D: See? That is what I mean. I think that may be the reason why J-Cob went back to women 100 percent—to rid himself of the pain and embarrassment you would have brought him. You have a serious issue, Jo-Joan, and it ain't from men using you. It is because you have anger, and it shows every day. I have been trying to let you see it for yourself, but all you do is ignore the truth and blame others. I do like being with you the way we get down, but I am starting to not feel you. In fact, I have become confused in so many ways as to what I want: a woman or you, who are a man, whether you choose to believe that or not.

Jo-Joan: I tell you this: my anger comes from being used by men and let go as though there is nothing about me but ass. I am a person, and I mean to be treated as such in life. I am not all about me. I am about us at this moment. But if you are starting to doubt yourself in the way you claim, I do feel that I might have to be the one to move on. I can't compete with a real woman. I want to ensure that you are happy, because I care for you. If you look at it closely, we have not had anything but a sexual escapade, and I do feel that I am more than that. Besides, there is one man for me in this life, and I am willing to move on. I think I have taken my pain out on you as a relief valve in life. J-Cob has always been on my mind. At times I pictured him with me. I know it was wrong, but I had no control of my feelings.

D: So you used me all this time and I didn't know it?

Jo-Joan: No, I didn't. I let you venture off because I needed to be sure of what I wanted. I know J-Cob still cares for me, as he has called me and told me of his feelings. You have had yours, and now you are complaining. Please, man, you can't have all you want in life. So if you are feeling confused, I think it is time for you to leave. I have to start getting myself together for the return of my J-Cob. I have waited two years, and I feel that I will be blessed soon in life.

D: Now Jo-Joan, I don't mean to be a bearer of bad news, but I do believe that J-Cob moved on from you. Now you sit here and say you and he have been creeping behind my back?

Jo-Joan; No. I said I have been talking to him off and on. He has just been a distant friend looking in on a friend, and that is all. Why are you tripping? It's over between us, as you say, so be gone, guy. I am willing to end this quietly, but you seem to care more than you admit.

D: I care for you, yes, but this life I lead is not right in the eyes of Good. Mia-Duke has talked and talked of believing and doing what is right. How do I really know if this is right? Only God will be my judge on that. I hope he forgives me in any way he can, because I know I am a good man, Jo-Joan. I am or feel I was just confused in life. I need to find my way, and it will start today. I really hope you can forgive me. I have to stop what we are doing and be completely straight up with you and myself. I have been interested in this one female that everybody knows, and I can't go to her with a lie in my heart. I have not made love to her, but Lord knows I want to. I am sleeping with you to fill a moment. I want to smile completely without looking over my back. I want to go out and explore the world of life with a person who wants to be with me. Jo-Joan, you want J-Cob, and I was just a moment. You and I know this won't work at all. I truly hope we can be friends, I mean distant friends in life, because this can't get out and I won't let it.

Now let's get it together and leave. Damn, do you have to use so much Chanel #5? My damn eyes are burning.

Jo-Joan: Shut up and let's go, boy. I know I smell good and I am good. That is why you have been hitting it for over two years. Stop smiling, my friend; it won't happen again. But I did care for you, D. I truly did or I would not have been with you this for so long. I hope you can forget all of this. (Laughs.)

D (laughing): Jo-Joan, please. You knew the deal. Now let me drop you off. I have a date and I am already running late.

CHAPTER 41

Renewal of Love

Chad: Hello, Kathy, and how are you feeling these days?

Kathy: I am fine. What made you place a call to me? I thought you were all about being a father to Lakeeba, and yet I have not heard from you at all in two years. I have just been taking it easy in life. And what have you been doing since that day, Chad?

Chad: I have been missing you.

Kathy: What are you talking about? Missing me? Please.

Chad: Kathy, I swear that I have been so lonely without you in my life. I am a lonely man and not by force—by choice. I have not been with a woman in over two years. Ever since Lakeeba and you came back into my life, I have concentrated on cleansing my soul.

Kathy: Is that so?

Chad: Yes, it is. I have waited so long to call you. I hoped that when I was free of the BS in life and cleansed that you would see me as the man you met years ago and try to work with me in this life.

Kathy: Chad, oh Chad, why are you doing this to me? I gave up on you years ago and lived a hurtful life. I wanted you to come and rescue me, but you never came. I had to endure so much pain from that lunatic. I cried night after night for you, Chad. I loved you so much. No matter what happened that made us not be together, I wanted to forget and get you back in my life. But over time I found you, and you were with another woman. Having two sons with her closed the book on my search to gain you again in life.

Chad: Then I wasn't wrong in assuming you were looking at me with love in your eyes that day we came to meet Lakeeba?

Kathy: I won't lie. No, you weren't wrong. I can admit that I still do love you, but you are a different man.

Chad: No. I am a changed man. I am just into the Lord and want so badly for you and me to meet him when he calls us home.

Kathy: Oh my God, you are changed. It sounds like you are.

Chad: Kathy, I love you, and I must have you in my life. I want to be a family: Jacob, Paul, Lakeeba, you, and I. One big, happy family. I know we can do this. I have never stopped loving you, and I will prove it every day to you. I promise I will, Kathy.

Kathy: I don't know. I mean, I have been single for some time now, I think longer than you, and not by force either but by choice. I felt that there was nothing out there for me but users in life, and I have been used enough, Chad.

Chad: I won't hurt you again. I swear on my grave that it will be you and I for life. We are both mature enough to know what we want. I have waited so many years away from my true love, and I want to make you happy for the rest of your life. I just need a chance to show you who I am, and that is not a thug but a real man. Kathy, I gave it all up years before I seen you and Lakeeba. Since that day, I've wanted nothing but to be the man you always wanted.

Kathy: As lonely as I am in life, my heart can't take being hurt again, especially by a man I had a child with years ago. I want to be happy and in love and provide for a man who loves me for me. But being this age, it won't happen.

Chad: Kathy, did you hear me or anything I said?

Kathy: I heard everything you said. I want you to know how much I want to take your every word, but you hurt me. (Crying:) Chad, you really hurt me.

Chad: I know, but please let me show you love, real love. I need you so much, and I won't have any woman unless it is you. You deserve everything I have, and it is yours. I love you and I want to show you, Kathy. Please hear me for what I am trying to say. I love you and I want to be the man I should have been in life. I just need a chance to show you. (Crying:) I have never forgiven myself for being so stupid and hurting you. I want to be your everything. I need for you to see me for who I have become. God has blessed me in so many ways. I know the light is shining, and he has guided my heart and restored me, his son. Please know I am a good man. I have been true to my God. I did wrong by so many and handled many in terrible ways, but I am changed in life. I never killed anyone, but I hurt many people, mainly by being a bully. Baby, I am calling to beg for your hand.

Kathy: My hand! What are you talking about?

Chad: I want to marry you and become one again in life. I know we can be so good to each other. I want to show you the world. I have so much to offer you, my love. And I am not buying your heart. I aim to travel and see the world, and I want to see it with you. Please know that I don't expect you to drop all and marry me, but at least let's get to know each other again and build a relationship.

Kathy: There you go, charming me all up. Chad, I am not about the money you have.

Chad: I know, and I am not about the money either. I have all I need to survive. I am about getting the woman I love.

Kathy: I have to be true in what I say to you. I have never stopped loving you, and I want to at least try to build. Let's start as associates, then friends, and then work from there. Okay?

Chad: I will take a flower as long as it belongs to you …

Kathy: So it's a date tomorrow?

Chad: Yes, Kathy, it is. I thank you. See you at eight tomorrow night.

Kathy: Why so late?

Chad: Because I want to keep you out as late as I can. Good night.

Kathy: Good night.

CHAPTER 42

CHEYENNE/SECRET INTEREST

Cheyenne: Hi, Derek. Where are you, boy? You were supposed to be here a minute ago.

Derek: I know, right? I had to take Maria home. She was talking and talking, and I didn't want her all in our business.

Cheyenne: Look, Derek, you and I are like fifth cousins, which to me don't exist at all. It's like my mother's friend and your mother's friend just hung out and now call themselves cousins. And on top of that, I just found out two years ago that May May was my mom. So you are my boo and that is that. So again, where are you?

Derek: Outside. Come on.

Derek gives Cheyenne a quick kiss and they drive off.

Cheyenne: Damn, don't your car smell with Maria's perfume? If she was not my cousin and in love with Paul,

I would have been jealous. But that is my girl, and it's cool. Even so, you are always looking out for others and not for me. I will get jealous about that, so chop-chop, boo-boo, and make it happen.

Derek: I will. When am I to get down with you? Hell, you and I have been dating for about four months, and all we do is cuddle and shit. You have your goodies on lock real tight.

Cheyenne: See? That is why I am still a virgin, because brothers like you still trip in life. When I think I am ready, you say some dumb shit and I lose all thoughts of giving myself to an asshole.

Derek: Okay, okay. I didn't mean it that way. I really want to be your first.

Cheyenne: You won't be anything but a memory, Derek. I like you and all, and I have always looked at you sideways. Then you come at me months ago, and here we are sneaking like you are or were scared all this time. Now today you seem all happy and on cloud nine like you are free. But as free as you feel, I am not going to be a cloud and let you use me. I have morals in life, and they will be fulfilled. I just need for you to relax and let it happen. If you keep on pressuring me, it won't. I did want you, but you are so different when it comes to chivalry. Show a lady some love, dude.

Derek: Look, young lady, I got you and it will happen soon. So how about you and I just enjoy our day?

Cheyenne: Wait, wait, wait! Now I know my cousin's perfume, and come to think of it, she doesn't like Chanel #5. She is a White Diamond girl. So who the hell you had up in here, dude? I knew I couldn't trust you. I am so glad I have common sense. You think I am a fool or something, Derek?

Derek: Girl, stop tripping. You are right; it wasn't Maria. It was a new friend of mine, because a man has got to get his, and you ain't ready to provide.

Cheyenne: So you are telling me that I kissed your ass in the mouth after you been slobbering on some other freak? Boy. Oh, man, you better be playing, Derek, or your ass gon' get slapped.

Derek: By whom? And by the way, little girl, get out of my car. When you get ready to be a woman, call me. Now get out, because you are tripping on me being me. The man you met. How long you want me to wait to hold you?

Cheyenne: Until I was to have married your ass, that's how long. Now carry your ass, because I am still pure and happy about it. I am glad God guided me right in my decisions. You can go and kick rocks, Mr. Hard Dick, because you ain't never getting at me with your nasty ass. You make me sick! (Opens the door, exits, and slams the door.) Bye, stupid dummy! Playing me, what kind of fool he thinks I am? Stupid dummy. Anyway I am out of here, so drive on, stupid dummy. I am so glad I have kept my legs closed. Ain't nothing but bullshitters here in life. Straight bullshitters.

CHAPTER 43

THE BOTTLE

Studae (stuttering): Tulip, man, why are you so foolish to revert back to drinking?

Tulip: Man, shut up, Studae, and work on your speech. I thought you were taking speech impediment classes or something.

Studae: I am, man. And I am doing great. I just lapse when I am mad. I am mad, Tulip. Shut up.

Tulip: Man, I said shut up. How do you expect me to go cold turkey in a week? I will get there with the Lord; I know I will. Just stick with me and don't let me go, Studae.

Studae (no longer stuttering): Stop! Stop! Stop, man and I mean stop, you damn fool. We prayed for help, and you are helping your damn self to more liquor. I mean stop. Put it down, Tulip, and do it now, before I whip your ass, you stubborn fool.

Tulip looks on in shock as Studae speaks freely. He is really in amazement and wants to hug his boy, but is stopped in his tracks as he walks up.

Studae: Stop right there, man, and put that damn bottle down. I mean do it *now*. I am not for disrespecting my Lord, and I won't stand by and let you do it. So you better make a choice before I make it for you. Now, as I was saying, try me.

Tulip: Man, if God is working at this moment, I am a witness to a miracle. You couldn't speak worth a dime. I mean, you were awful. I mean, you were a joke, I mean—

Studae: Shut up and do as I say, man.

Tulip (crying): Man, how can I just let it go? I have been drinking for half my life. It is a part of my blood. I want to be able to smile at you with fresh breath daily, but I can't just walk away. Counseling has not helped much, and all you do is pray. Big Bo, he prays; Grahams prays; and so on. The whole family prays, and I am the one who is still sick. Oh my God, help me … I need you but I can't stop. God help me.

Studae (runs to his boy and grabs him as he faints in his arms, crying): I got you, Tulip. The Lord and his tribe have you, my friend. I will be by your side. Lord, please guide my friend and me into your arms, showing us the way, God. We need you more than ever. I want you to know that I see it, I know it, and I feel it, God. I am not free, but I am working. I need you more than ever. You have given me the strength to speak freely, and I thank you, God. I am sorry for playing with Tulip, in that I learned to speak freely months ago with your help. I just had to use you, as you say we should in life. You are there for me, and I will be there for you. I am free, Lord, and I will stand by Tulip. The family knew he would struggle, but we have him, Lord. I pray these words to you, my father. Thank you. Amen. Amen, amen, amen!

When you have an interest in someone

You must follow your unforeseen notions that guide your inner inhibitions from one zone to another ... Therefore, when your wish becomes your want, your interest has become involved ... Now when one becomes involved, one must control all aspects of the situation. Think about a want before it becomes a need. When a need has crossed the threshold of a need, it states that you're involved ...

See, this letter is written to explore the mind, and your mind is mine.

Meeting someone who is a mystery can only enhance your motives to approach, and when you approach that person; he or she will always remain in your heart. You may not have the opportunity to conquer that soul, but that soul is available. In time, some have wanted so much, and when we have had that taste of another's juices, we often look for ways to create a noble following. Take all that's offered and indulge in one's feast. Too often we lose control of the most sensitive urges that tell of the truth. And often the truth will hurt if you're not prepared. Are you?

And the story read.

Intentions are wearing thin on my feelings, and the touch is within my grasp. Can you make it happen, or will you continue to deny your needs, wants, and intentions/

Make it happen and enjoy the richness of my moisture. Enjoy the scent of my aroma, and most definitely enjoy the strength of my touch … Make it happen.

Now? Where do we stand? Better yet, what do you want?

If you have had an interest, why did you not be the woman I know you are and a make the move with caution? My bite would not have hurt. To tell you the truth, I would have been flattered. You are a special person with much to offer to a person who has the opportunity to hold you. But if you continue to run for your wants, you will always say, "Man, I should have …" Now again, what am I saying? I am saying that your intentions were mine all along, and if the day comes for us to explore each other, we should not be disappointed.

Now I am laying it on the line, and you should also. But I know caution is a major factor, and you have proven yourself to be very protective of your privacy and your heart. I am not one to hurt your heart, and I am not one to try and win it.

I am in a situation that you should understand and accept, and hopefully all will be understood. Take no side steps from the truth. If you want it, go for it, but if you don't, control it. A friendship is always a great thing. If you cross that point, it becomes a thing full of emotions. Finally, all I have to say is to make it happen if you want. But if your intention is only a child's game, then let it be. Once again, I want it only if you do. But truly, understand our positions …

CHAPTER 44

SURPRISES

The doorbell rings.

Grahams: Who is there?

Wellington Mitchell: Mr. Mitchell that is, and I would like for you to open the door, miss.

Grahams: Mr. Mitchell? I don't know any Mitchell, sir, and I won't be opening my door. (Peeking through the window:) OMG! Wellington Mitchell!

Opening the door slowly, Grahams is all smiles as she sees a former lover of hers who moved away ten years ago.

Grahams: Well, well. What brings you here, Welly?

Welly: You, my dear. I have been living away from you and missed New Orleans so much, I have returned. Now, gal, is there a man around who has stolen you away from me? Because I can't take any punches anymore. (Laughs.)

Grahams: Nah, man, and you are not here to reclaim your lost love, ya know?

Welly: Nah. I am here to see you and talk to you. I know it had been a long time. When I ran into Wilma, she told me that you were looking some good and I better get up to see you. I must admit, she didn't lie, Grahams. You are still as beautiful as the day you stood on the porch as I drove away from you. I have always regretted moving away. I had me a gal there, but it didn't work out. She was so settled in her nasty ways that it was a shame. But I am here now to talk to my old friend. Grahams, talk to me.

Grahams: The Lord God is the only thing keeping me from bashing you in the head, man. How you going to come here smiling like you did nothing wrong after breaking my heart? You old fool.

Welly: Why, I thought you were happy to see me, smiling and all.

Grahams: Nah. I was happy the Lord was with me and I smiled from not slapping you silly. You have no right to show up here. I wonder what your deal is, man. You are always running for something, but I ain't got nothing to offer but advice. Give the Lord a chance, mister. Now be gone or be lost, old man. Oh, I am sorry. Mr. Wellington Mitchell.

Grahams walks away, singing "God Blessed Me" and smiling. Welly grabs his belongings and heads to the door with a WTF look on his face. He's been shot down by yet another woman in life who figured him out. He was after money, and when it ran out, he was out. But today he didn't want to be out quickly. He has a plan, and Grahams intends to find out what it is. She knows he will be back soon, very soon.

Welly drives away smiling. He thinks he's played it off really well, and he has a plan to get close to the money that is rumored to be in the family. He has an idea that Grahams has the lead in this and wants to get close to get some cash. But how can he get in when he doesn't fit in anymore? He is a player and left Grahams for another woman with cash. She died, and he used the entire fund living a lavish lifestyle. Now he needs some money to get back to the way he lived—like a movie star. But it will be a hard task to get something from Grahams.

It is a shame that Wilma still has a big mouth. She told Welly that Grahams was well off in life. The only thing Welly really knows is that Grahams mentioned something to Wilma about her future without any headaches, and Wilma told Welly that Grahams didn't need for anything. Welly took that as a sign of being well off or having come into some money, some way, somehow. But oh, how he will be played in the end.

CHAPTER 45

DETECTIVE DAVID DICKENS AND MAY MAY

Cheyenne comes inside, fuming.

Cheyenne: May May, you in here? I need to talk. May May, where are you?

She finds Detective David Dickens and May May hugged up on the sofa in Grahams's living room.

Cheyenne: Oh, excuse me! I am so sorry for barging in like this.

May May: It is okay. I thought you left for that date of yours. Why are you back so soon?

Cheyenne: Straight dog, May May, I mean he had the nerve to pull up to get me with all kinds of female fragrance inside his car, like I am a fool. I was like, oh, no way am I going to let this fool use me. And Mom, I mean May May, I really liked him.

May May: Now I caught that, Cheyenne. There is no need not to feel comfortable calling me Mom. I am your mom, and I am okay with you saying it. Okay, baby?

Cheyenne: Yes, ma'am. I know, but I have been trying not to because I didn't want my mom who raised me to feel bad.

May May: Love, we talked of that and she is okay with us both being Mom to you. I love you and I always have, baby. Please, no more apologies for that. Just call me Momma May May when Carroll and I are around.

Cheyenne: Okay, Momma May May. And who, might I ask, is this gentleman all up in my mom's face?

David stands.

David: Hi, young lady, and how are you? I am David, a good friend of your mom's, and I have been waiting to formally meet you. I hope all else is well for you, even though your date turned out to be playing games with your heart. Believe me, it will be okay. Anyway, your mom and I have known each other for, let's say, some three years. I am so fond of her. In fact, I can say it to the world. I am in love with your mom. May May, I love you.

May May (crying): Oh my God, I love you too, David. I just didn't know how to tell you. I have loved you from the day of our first kiss. You are such a man, and I am so proud to be dating you.

Cheyenne: Wait, wait, I thought you said you were a dear friend, and now the truth? So you two have been dating each other for this long and no one knows about it at all. You two are professional sneakers. (Laughs.) But Mom, he seems to be a great catch. I mean, daddy material. So, Mister David, are you planning something here in the future?

David: Yes, I am. I want to step back and take my place with you here, Cheyenne.

Cheyenne: OMG! No, you are not, sir. Oooh, Mom … Oooh … *Grahams*!

Grahams comes in from her room, running, and finds David on his knees and May May in tears.

Grahams: May May, child, what is going on and why are you crying?

May May points to David, who is crying and holding a beautiful diamond ring in his hands.

David: May May, you and I have been an item for over two years. There is no need to play around in life any longer without you being my wife. I love you so much. Please do me the honor of being my wife.

May May: OMG! Is this real?

David: Real as it can ever be in life. I want you as my wife, and I will have it no other way. I love you. Now am

I to sit here with tears in my face, my arms hurting, and my knees about to break? Please answer in between those beautiful tears.

Grahams: Girl, please shut up for a minute and answer this charming fella …

May May: Yes, ma'am. David, yes, I will, for I have loved you and loved you and now the world can share in our love. OMG! I am getting married! Thank you, Jesus!

Grahams: Hallelujah …

May May and David kiss and are joined by Grahams and Cheyenne as they all say a little prayer and thank God for his blessing.

CHAPTER 46

PAUL AND MARIA

Southern University at New Orleans (SUNO):

Maria: Paul, who is this one chick Val that keeps you lit up all the time? I seem to be in competition for your heart with this fool. Please fill me in because I am lost, and lost you will be if you are playing me.

Paul: Baby girl, who are you tripping? You know we have been together from the start. Ain't no other lady stepping in on us. So why all the noise? You have been listening to all of your friends who want your happiness, I see. But you have to be strong or lose out in life. All of those chicks hang on for one thing that is being passed around, and that is that you are paid. I don't know where that notice is coming from, because I am the man and I handle all of the bills when we go out.

Maria: Wait, wait, Paul. I take care of you, and I am not only talking physically. I mean take care of you. You have on gear I bought, and look at those shoes. You know that is my style, so don't trip.

Paul: Baby, I didn't say that. I said that I am the man and I handle my business as a man, so they shouldn't be tossing rumors around that you are paid. That info might get in the hands of the wrong people, and then my baby can be subject to an issue I don't want to handle now in life. I am a hothead, and I will hurt someone over my baby. You heard me?

Maria: I heard ya, but it ain't that type of party. And also, if I was paid, I would be rolling and not with munchies in my face. I would not be here at SUNO; I would be at Penn State or something far away from the bullshit. Baby knows that I am with you, and we are doing this together. I want to be with only you, and it will happen, love. Believe me in that. I will have you and only you as my husband. I truly love you, Paul, and it has been proven over and over in life.

Paul: I know, right? You and I have been on top of the world with each other. I love you so much, girl, but you have to stop tripping and make it about you and I all the time. I only said a few words to Val the other day at the game, and your girl Carla was all in our mess, talking about "I see you, Paul." I told her to beat it and to stop tripping. She walked off with an attitude, and that is why I knew it was her from the start.

Maria: You and I are soon to be twenty-one years old, and we don't need drama. We need God and our love. I know it is hard for people to date for so long and then marry and stay committed to each other in this world, but we have got to believe we can do this. I for one don't see anything out there for me but you and me as one. You heard me?

Paul I heard ya, girl. Now come here and kiss me. (Laughs.) Now Maria, what is all this noise about you being rich and stuff? I mean, people are whispering all this noise, and I don't have a clue. You and I left for college and dated for years. I don't get where it is coming from other than someone trying to play jokes. It is becoming a nuisance and not a joke.

Maria: I don't know, Paul.

She hugs him. The worried look on her face shows that she wonders where all this is coming from now after two years of keeping quiet.

CHAPTER 47

THE MONEY

Two years ago, at the final meeting before everyone left BJ's home so she could talk to Travis.

David: Okay, guys. First of all, congratulations on a job well done. It was an awesome display of professionalism on everyone's part. But I have to say this: never think about that life again. It was a moment to help bring down a bunch of rapists who happened to be rich in life. People are so sick in this world and they got what they were doing.

Marcia: Thank you, Lord, for that. Yes, Lord!

Everyone: Amen.

David: There is one problem that we may have to deal, with but maybe not if you hear me out closely. And I mean please listen. One of the johns we captured is the son of the former governor. He means business. He has connections and wants his son off the hook for this, but I won't deal. I want his head, and I will have it. I just want you all to know everything and not just a part of what is going on. This case is very serious. It is carrying a lot of weight, and heads will roll. They have even threatened my boss, the commissioner. He is upset that I didn't let him in on the bust, but it will be okay. This will go to trial, and it will take time, but we will get them. Then we have an issue that pertains to the money. As you know, it was supposed to be seven million, but it turned out to be ten million. We used three million to pay everyone who was involved to remain quiet, and they also have to wait for their payouts.

Grahams: Son, if that is the case, we don't want any money. We want our happiness and our God. Yes, Lord, bless us; yes, Lord, bless us. Now, I told you I didn't want these girls to have no issues with this. You promised me, and now you are telling us this.

David: Right you are, Ms. Grahams. I did say that, and I had the plans worked out from the start. I want you to hear me clearly. Please, no more interruptions while I lay it out. First, no one will touch the funds for three years. That way you won't be tied to this case. The men have been spilling beans about four young ladies having money of theirs and playing a part in setting them up. So if you are out there bling bling all over town, you will be marked and taken out like that. The three million will be used in part to hire decoys to spend the cash. That way, we will create a mirage for those who have their eyes on the young ladies with the money. We will used $1.5 million to get this done. I need you to all be in agreement. I will pay at least thirty women to just live it up with no comment. I will go out and recruit with a disguise, and it will work. The ladies will be happy to be dressing and doing the thing all for free. When the nasties have all been locked away for two years, we will make our move on the funds, and no one will be able to track a thing. I think it will work, and it will be like a savings account for the young ladies. When questions arise about their lifestyles, the answers will lie with me. And I ain't talking to no one but the lawyers who are trying the case.

BJ: Well seems to me like you have it all worked out. I have no issues with waiting, as I have been employed and know how to manage my life. So you said you had seven million left, and my question is how will this be distributed?

David: Well, each of you girls will receive one million apiece, and Marcia will receive a million for her great work. The other one million will go to a secret partner who helped me with this case. She has been very productive in many setups and is a beautiful woman to me, if I may add. Now my cut in this is nothing. I am the law, and it is on my side. But I will use the last million dollars to put those creeps in jail for life.

Maria, Shay, Dee Dee, and BJ all smile as they eat and laugh. The doorbell rings, and it is Travis. BJ knows that life will be great from here on out. Her smiles have been truly restored.

CHAPTER 48

JONE'T

Jone't: I tell you this: Father will be free soon, and I promise you that, Janel. Yeah, I know he was screwing all types of women and doing wrong in some ways, but the damn mommas who sold their kids are not even being punished. It's like hell what they did, and the cops just make the man pay for the pain that the mother provided as well? I mean, a man will be a man, and that is why I can't stand men for nothing but one thing, and that is to use them like they use us. I may be a ho in life to many, but to me, I am getting mine, girl.

Janel: Girl, I can't say too much, but I will say this: you ain't never lying, because Calvin, Jerome, and Miller are always in my face, trying to get something to eat. I play these fools like Play-Doh every time, and they know it. But because they are stupid-ass men, tail will drive their behinds crazy. They will put up with any shit I throw at them, and that is no lie. But tell me how you are going to work your plan.

Jone't: I am working all the parameters right now. My dad told me he knows that Marcia set them up, and she will pay dearly. She will pay … I mean, if my dad has to do life, a life will have to be given. I am not talking killing anyone; I am talking their asses going to jail also. But mainly my pops is working this thing for a technicality, because he didn't pay for sex. The other fools brought their money to the scene, but my pops was suspicious of their little asses coming on the scene all bold and shit.

Janel: Girl, I can't believe how they set your pops and them all up so good. Now most of those men in their fifties ain't getting out and will rot in there all alone. But they are rich going in so maybe they can hire whoever to protect them while they are locked up.

Jone't: Girl, it ain't even about those nasty-ass old men, including my dad. It is about that money my pops has locked down and ain't about to part with. No matter if he stays in or gets out, he ain't signing shit. I want him out because I am richer with him out than in. He has me on a strict plan, and that includes not taking over his businesses. But I got plans, girl; I got plans. Now watch me work it for ya.

Janel: Well, whatever you do, I got you and I am down, my chick. I need to get paid, and I will work for mine; you can believe that. Hell, I lie on my ass for free; I might as well get really paid.

Jone't: I mean, just look at them parade around like nothing never happened, and to use those fakes at the trial was marvelous but oh so wrong. My father's lawyer said over and over that the film was doctored. When the camera was about to present a face, it suddenly cut off. I know it was that sometimes-dyke bitch BJ who is all in love with a dude now. But all will come out. Her parade will be stopped in the street she walks on, and that is for sure. They just don't know that money speaks volumes, and we know the truth and the whole plan. Detective Dickens will pay with his job. That promotion will be out of the window and gone like his ass when my pops gets out. Like I said, money speaks volumes, and people will kill for theirs in life. Like the old movie went, *Rock-A-Bye Baby*! (Laughs maniacally.)

Janel is now paranoid, as she has just implicated herself in a devious plan that may include killing someone—a detective was not part of her plans at all. She wanted to get paid, but now she wants out. However, she knows too much. Knowing how stupid Jone't is, she has to sneak out of the plan. And she will, one way or the other.

Janel: Girl, you are tripping if you are talking about murder.

Jone't: It won't be murder; it will be payback in the line of self-defense, and I will be the star player of this movie. Just watch …

Janel: Look, Jone't, it is all right and dandy to help your pops and get paid, but no one was out to kill anyone.

Jone't: Girl, I am to do what I have to do, and that is get paid and live my life treating stupid-ass men the way they deserve to be treated, and that is like a dirty dog. I will get mine, and that is that.

Janel (scared but laughing): You are a trip, girl, but I got you. I got you. So tell me, Jone't, what is the plan?

CHAPTER 49

PEP AND TULIP

Pep: Unk, you know I watch you daily, or at least every time I come around, and it seems as if you have it together. I mean, I see how you come at people, and although you had a problem, you seem to rise above the distractions of life. It is like you can resist the temptation of life. Yet there are many people in the world today who can't resist or avoid trouble.

Tulip: See, young man, it comes from experience in life. But mainly from our teaching in life. It started years ago as far as resisting change in life. Let me break it down to you, son. You do have a minute, right?

Pep: I am here, Unk.

Tulip: In life, to be held captive and forced to provide free labor would cause anyone to have for the leaders of the negative world. The whippings, forced religion, new names, rape, torture, and decapitation would change one from calm to dangerous and the inevitable, death. That alone was reason to rebel against the fake leaders of the sacred or so-called negative land. I want to tell you about the word *resistance.*

The British viewed resistance as economic advancement, selling slaves for profit prior to issuing strict laws against such acts. The owning of slaves was vital to the development of the world. Slaves of masters would work for nothing and had no choice in the matter. They were basically forced to provide unlimited support to the production affairs of their slave masters. Although there were laws created to protect the slaves, they were rarely followed. The native Indians were first used in the labor process in South America, Jamaica, and the Caribbean, only to be replaced gradually by the slaves, with whom they worked solidly side by side in the beginning.

In the 1850s, the slave states, which had already become a minority in the House of Representatives, were facing a future as a perpetual minority against an increasingly powerful North. Therefore, if you take a look at control, you would point to the political market as saying that the price of life can be bought on all levels, and especially in politics. Every slave owner prospered in life, as was evident in the overall development of their land.

Some of the slaves had been kings and queens in their native villages of Africa. Now they were thrown to the wolves and placed in chains, neck braces, spikes, thorns and other humiliating devices. That would cause anyone to lose it, let alone a human being of royalty.

In the eyes of the slave master, if you were not of Caucasian descent, you were nothing but a worker on their behalf. Life is never sweet unless you demand the right to be treated fairly, and in those times, fairness was of the essence. You had nowhere to go, living far away from your homeland, taken captive, and placed in unsanitary conditions. Placed in front of your future owners, naked at times on display. Your scars hidden with tar and your mind in disarray. How could a man or woman forced into those living conditions function normally under the leadership of a slave owner?

In reading the work of the famous African Americans, I can only imagine how it felt to be told the untruth. In the mid-1800s the NAACP, was formed to better serve the African American nation, only to be challenged in the year 1905 by the famed W. E. B. Dubois and William Monroe Trotter, who themselves formed the Niagara Movement. Although meaningful in what it was trying to accomplish, the Niagara Movement came to a stalemate in the year 1910 without financial support. The Red Summer of the year 1919 was devastating in East St. Louis. Numerous riots wreaked havoc and proved to be detrimental to the growth of black people. To think that we had to endure so much hatred and feared for our freedom is strictly unbelievable.

The famous boxer Jack Johnson was a signified example of hatred for a black man. He won the heavyweight championship of the world. His fame was tainted by his choice to date white woman and flaunt it in the face of white America. After he won the title, white America looked to the retired Jack Dempsey to proclaim their right to supremacy. "The Great White Hope," as he was called, failed in that attempt, which only sent the white nation into anger all across America, killing numerous people in the process.

The Great Migration between the years 1916 to 1918 was vital to the continuing growth of black people of America. In Chicago alone, population of black people increased 150 percent by the year 1920. In retrospect, life for all changed with the development of the protected order of the organizations that formed in the 1800s.

Some of the topics that were very important to the Niagara Movement and the NAACP were that in order to fight for the right of equal treatment, one had to be very knowledgeable about what one chose to defend. In winning a case of grievance, the NAACP scored an early success in 1915. A Supreme Court decision outlawed the grandfather clause that had restricted black suffrage.

Decades later, we still continue to see justice in our favor, such as the landmark case of Brown vs. Board of Education in 1954. And in today's society, the work of those great African Americans has proven evident in all the accolades we continue to receive and the goals we continuously achieve. I am one to always state the phrase that "Life is written, and the way our lives are played out has been decided by the One above." Our fight for equal rights has been a long and stressful journey, but no matter what, I truly feel that we as African American people will reap the rewards awaiting us all in life.

Pep: Unk, you are one deep brother. I may have to take you with me to talk to a few fools who just don't get it. I don't think they will be able to sit calmly, but at least I know you will get their attention. And that is simply because you are Uncle Tulip Melbourne …

FINAL WORDS

Grahams: See, children? The Lord has plans, and his plans have been laid out for us all to follow. Whenever you think you have it going on, slow down. Look up and say thank you. Wake up and say thank you. Sit at his table and remember to say thank you. Throughout the day, look up and say thank you to him for allowing you to live another day. When you lay it down, say thank you, and when you get up, say thank you.

Danger is all around us daily, and we never take a moment to say thank you. Praise the One who has provided you with nothing but happiness. Your happiness is my happiness, and my happiness comes from my Lord.

Smile, children. Look up and say it with me: *thank you*!

QUOTES OF LIFE

- Smiles are meant to enlighten the heart. Have you smiled today?
- The sky is only high if your goals are unreachable.
- The true spirit is the given thought. Think before you act.
- Knowledge is not wasted if applied in life.
- Outer beauty uplifts us all, but inner beauty helps us survive. What do you possess?
- When you have lost the consciousness of respect for our ancestors, you have lost in life.
- If you forget what others have fought for in life, you have lost in life.
- Don't forget what others fought for in life, and that is not stupidity.
- If you give up in life, you give up on others, and therefore you give up on God.
- Live out your script, for life is written.
- The Devil failed you, your family loved you, and God saved you.
- Appreciate you, live you, love you, and it will help you appreciate others.

—Troy Palmer

SELECTED BIBLIOGRAPHY

Baskerville, Stephen. "The Myth of Deadbeat Dads." *Liberty Magazine*, June 2002. Republished by Equal Justice Foundation. http://www.ejfi.org/family/family-60.htm.

Beringer, Richard E., Herman Hattaway, Archer Jones, and William N. Still Jr. *Why the South Lost the Civil War.* Athens: University of Georgia Press, 1991.

Beringer, Richard E., Herman Hattaway, Archer Jones, and William N. Still Jr. *The Elements of Confederate Defeat: Nationalism, War Aims, and Religion.* Athens: University of Georgia Press, 1988.

Ellison, Ralph. *The Invisible Man.* New York: Vintage, 1995.

Mullane, Deirdre. *Crossing the Danger Water: Three Hundred Years of African-American Writing.* New York: Anchor Books, 1993.

Kelley, Robin D.G. and Earl Lewis. *To Make Our World Anew: The History of African Americans.* New York: Oxford University Press, 2000.

Walker, Bruce. "Deadbeat Dads? Look Closer." The Christian Science Monitor, August 16, 1996. http://www.csmonitor.com/1996/0816/081696.opin.opin.3.html.

Wikipedia. "Atlantic slave trade." http://en.wikipedia.org/wiki/Atlantic_slave_trade.

A LOOK AHEAD AT REALITY OF LIFE: BOOK 2

The entire family begins to look into the future.

Maria leaves Paul for the big life of a star once the money comes in.

Paul meets Lakeeba's cousin, Tabitha, and dates her happily.

Shay and Tim split and get back together over and over, but she quietly accepts BJ's life.

May May builds a great relationship with her daughter Cheyenne and marries David Dickens.

Raul becomes a minister.

Pep and Mike open a restaurant.

Dee and Nicole open a beauty salon.

Nicole falls in love with the big life and forgets those in her past, including Bobby and the salon.

Giselle marries a wealthy businessman who is the cousin of one of the nasty crew, who are jail.

Studae learns to speak without stuttering, falls in love, and has a kid.

Jesus and Lakeeba continue dating, but Lakeeba's eyes are widening at a newcomer to town, Justin.

Derek opens a car business and stays straight. His secret never gets out to those who know him.

There has been a technical violation in the set-up bust. One of the convicted millionaires is set to be released unless BJ comes forward and testifies. BJ doesn't want her identity known, as it will bring pain to her newfound relationship with her mother, Marcia.

Jone't, the outsider and the headache, is the cause of a great secret.

J-Cob wants to be with Jo-Joan on the down low but wants it strictly between them.

The Pregnancy

Grahams is always on point, with more to clean up for the family.

ABOUT THE AUTHOR

Troy Lynn Palmer is the name I was born with on March 22, 1967, at 0201 hours in Charity Hospital, New Orleans, Louisiana, to my parents March E. Palmer and Mortie A. Forman. In my life I have accomplished many great things and seen a lot, but no matter the obstacles or the adversity I faced in life, I made it. My parents produced twelve children, together and apart.

I graduated in 1986 from Walter L. Cohen Senior High School, where I played tight end and defensive end for the Green Hornets football team. I worked numerous jobs for two years, including garbage man, landscaper, and Popeye's Fried Chicken employee. It was rough, but I did what I had to do to become a man in New Orleans.

I enlisted in the military on June 16, 1986, at the age of nineteen. On March 5, 1987, fifteen days prior to my twentieth birthday, I headed off to the Great Lakes to begin boot camp. I graduated and finished ATD School, and four months later, I was off to Little Creek Amphibious Base in Norfolk, Virginia. My first ship was the USS *Sumpter* LST 1181. I finished my great career on board the USS *George H. W. Bush* CVN 77, where I retired. I served twenty-six outstanding years with no major infractions.

I am married to my beautiful wife Me'Linda R. (Mills) Palmer. I have two children with my first wife, Marcus Troy Palmer and Empris Ramona Palmer, and one stepdaughter, Jakia Mon'e Teasley.

During my navy career, I received many accolades and accomplished tremendously. The one thing I am most proud of is the fact that I lived and am living a free and clean life. To me it is my duty, my mission, my honor, and, of course, my calling to live a good life. Growing up in the world, that is not easy. As we all face adversity, day in and day out, we have to remain free from all the negative qualities in life.

I believe that all good given comes back to the one who gave to others. I am a giver in life, at least with my knowledge and strength. It is about how you present yourself. The people who have a chance to meet you will have great things to say of you unless you have not lived a good life.

I first wrote a play called *Reality of Life: Maria* in 2000 while on a major deployment with the USS *Harry S Truman* CVN 75. That play was written and rewritten repeatedly. During my final seven-month deployment, I decided to turn the play into a book. By the time I returned to my home port of Norfolk, Virginia, I had completed six books.